# A MURDER MYSTERY

Best wishes Boots

George M. Bauer

# OTHER BOOKS FROM MARQUETTE BOOKS

John Wheeler, *Last Man Out: Memoirs of the Last Associated Press Reporter Kicked Out of Castro's Cold-War Cuba* (forthcoming 2008). ISBN: 978-0-922993-84-0

Steve Hallock, *"War Stories" from Great American Journalists of the Late 20th Century* (forthcoming 2008). ISBN: 978-0-922993-85-7

Dan Robison, *Death Chant: Kimo's Battle with the Shamanic Forces* (2006). ISBN: 0-922993-52-1

Phil Tichenor, *Athena's Forum: A Historical Novel* (2006). ISBN: 0-922993-51-3

Melvin DeFleur, *A Return to Innocence: A Novel* (2006). ISBN: 0-922993-50-5

Ronald E. Goetz, *The Kid: A Novel about Billy the Kid's Early Years* (2005). ISBN: 0-922993-20-3

Dan Robison, *Death Chant: Kimo Battles the Shamanic Forces* (2006). ISBN: 0-922993-52-1

Dan Robison, *Kimo's Escape: The Story of a Hawaiian Boy Who Learns to Believe in Himself* (2005). ISBN: 0-922993-28-9

Dan Robison, *Wind Seer: The Story of One Native American Boy's Contribution to the Anasazi Culture* (2005). ISBN: 0-922993-27-0

Ray Edwards, *Justice Never Sleeps: A Novel of Murder and Revenge in Spokane* (2005). ISBN: 0-922993-26-2

C. W. Burbank, *Beyond Zenke's Gate* (2004). ISBN: 0-922993-14-9

David Demers, *China Girl: One Man's Adoption Story* (2004). ISBN: 0-922993-08-4

# JACKLEG
## A MURDER MYSTERY

## GEORGE M. BAUCUM

MARQUETTE BOOKS LLC
SPOKANE, WASHINGTON

Copyright © 2008 by George M. Baucum

Printed in the United States of America

**Marquette Books Cataloging-in-Publication Data**

Baucum, George M., 1932-
Jackleg : a mystery novel / George M. Baucum.
p. cm.
ISBN-13: 978-0-922993-16-1 (pbk. : alk. paper)
1. Police--Fiction. I. Title.


Library of Congress Control Number: 2007939650




**MARQUETTE BOOKS**
3107 E. 62$^{nd}$ Avenue
Spokane, WA 99223
509-443-7057
books@marquettebooks.com
www.MarquetteBooks.com

# CHAPTER 1

"What's goin' on at the newspaper office, Riley?"

"I guess the biggest news is that Missy had a litter of kittens over the weekend. She's a heck of a mouser, but I don't think we need five of them. They're gonna put me in the poor house just feedin' 'em. I don't know why I ever took her in the first place. She just showed up one day and has been there ever since. Now she's been out tom cattin' around."

"Those things happen, you know."

"Yeah. I got her an orange crate and made a bed out of it. I put it over by the Linotype so she can keep warm. I don't know much about cats or how long it will take them to get weaned, but I know you're gonna want a couple."

"Yeah. You know it. Another cup of coffee?"

"Sure Mabel. As cold as it is, it's good coffee weather."

Riley finished his coffee and put the usual dime on the counter, five cents for the coffee and five cents for Mabel. "Guess I'd better go. I've got to drop by the funeral home and get the obit information on old man Westbrook. As slow as things are around this town, someone has to die before we have any news to print. See ya' later, Mabel."

Riley Hughes couldn't remember any time he wasn't involved in a newspaper. His father was editor, publisher, Linotype operator and printer as far back as Riley could recall. His mother worked three days a week gathering news, and Riley had his own pallet beside his mother. "Idle hands are the work of the devil," so said his father, and he was sure to see that Riley would not fall under the influence of Satin.

The *Weekly Standard* was anything but America's greatest economic enterprise, but it provided a living for the Hughes family. Until his father's retirement three years past, the front page sported

*"The Grapevine"* in which his father expounded on everything from broken shoelaces to international politics. Riley often wondered where his father came up with such a name; there wasn't a grapevine within two hundred miles.

Riley's mother worked two years after the old gent retired, and Riley hired Sara Ingram to take her place. Sara knew everyone in town, as well as everyone's dogs and cats. Not much escaped her, and she was constantly on the phone gathering news. Most of page two was taken up with "Mr. and Mrs. So and So went Somewhere to see Somebody" or "John Brown from back east is visiting his grandparents." Sara delighted in weddings and wedding anniversaries. She never omitted the slightest detail, even if it was something as inconsequential as cheese and celery sticks.

"Only one death this week, eh Tom?"

"So far."

"I see where Melody Collins and Susie Stern had their babies this past week, so we're gainin' on it."

"Yeah. I'm gonna miss old Charlie Westbrook. We played many a game of dominos. But I guess we all gotta go sometime. Here's the information on him. About the only family he had left was a sister living in Midland, Texas, and she's in a rest home."

Tom Smart was one of three classmates who remained in Ryan after graduation. Both Tom and Riley took over their fathers' businesses. Maurine Chastain was the only other one. Like Riley, she never married. She was a long way from a raving beauty and had a matching personality.

Riley stopped by Ben Armstrong's grocery long enough to pick up his weekly grocery ad plus a few cans of cat food for Missy. He ambled back to the newspaper office to find Sara on the phone. Sara was ideal for gathering the society news, what little there was, and Riley knew of no one who enjoyed talking more. Maybe gossiping would be better terminology.

Missy's four kittens were nursing as Riley sat the cans of cat food on the paper cutter. Missy sensed something good was about to happen and left her charges to themselves. She rubbed against Riley's leg and purred as he opened a can of Cat Food Delight.

"Here it is, girl, but if I see a mouse around here today I'm gonna cut your rations."

More often than not, Mondays were slow days in a weekly newspaper. Riley sat in his usual cushioned chair at the Linotype. He would set type on the obituary of Charlie Westbrook, the county agent's report released the previous Friday, anything that came out of the governor's office and whatever Sara had spiked on the copy hook. Never quite sure what advertising and want ads would come down the pike, Riley knew to have plenty of canned material on hand to fill any voids in the paper. He had several galleys of recipes, gardening tips, fishing information and a potpourri of similar articles.

Not being blessed with an abundance of type sizes on the Linotype, grocery ads and others requiring larger type for sale items required considerable handset type.

Tuesdays would be spent up and down Main Street calling on advertisers and the work would begin in earnest. Sara would be burning up the phone lines, calling the sheriff's office in the county seat, the local school system and the churches. No weekly paper would be complete or well received without the obituaries, church news, social news, school news or the sheriff's report.

The hand-fed press would print four pages at a time. It "came with the shop" as the elder Hughes said. Built just after the turn of the century, the old press rattled and moaned as Riley printed the first four pages as he usually did Wednesday night. He would print the other side Thursday morning, feed it through the folder and stamp the papers with an antiquated mailing machine. The papers would be delivered to the post office by two o'clock without fail.

Friday would be the day for printing letterheads, envelopes, statements and other orders. Seldom did it call for a full day's work, except during campaign season, when candidates would order campaign cards and placards. Riley would make his usual Friday evening call to Joyce Reid. Joyce worked at the variety store in Beaver Valley and lived in the small rural community of Madden Grove, halfway between Ryan and Beaver Valley. He would make arrangements to pick her up at six o'clock Saturday after the variety store closed. They would have dinner at the Casino Café and take in a movie at the Empress Theater. After the movie Riley would follow her to her home in Madden Grove.

Their relationship seemed to be based more on biology than anything else. Joyce's first husband left for "greener pastures," as Joyce jokingly said. "He wasn't much good at anything, and he sure wasn't the lady killer he thought he was." Husband Number Two was of the common law variety and, according to Joyce, he wasn't much better.

Riley had no plans to become Number Three. It was more or less a relationship of need and convenience and they both seemed satisfied to let it remain at that. It wasn't a secret, yet it was nothing either advertised except for the benefit of Joyce's neighbors.

Madden Grove had once been a bustling community of some two hundred residents. It sported a small depot, school, bank, one café, grocery store and a feed store. But once upon a time was just that, once upon a time. The highway was routed around Madden Grove in the late 1930s and all but killed any hope it had for future development. Most of its citizens had long since parted. Old Highway 81 was no more than a gravel road and a rough one at that. The school was closed in 1950, and students were bused into either Beaver Valley or Ryan.

Raised by her grandparents, Joyce Reid had inherited the old homestead. As with most of the remainder of Madden Grove, the old house could use considerable repair. Several homes had long since been abandoned and stood empty as reminders of what used to be.

Joyce was blessed with several nosey neighbors, none of whom approved of her less than straight and narrow lifestyle. Sybil Lang lived across the street and seldom missed anything. She was a fountain of knowledge concerning the happenings at Joyce's house.

The old lady once called the postmaster in Beaver Valley to report that the mailman had a young blonde female riding with him as he was delivering mail. She was disappointed to hear the postmaster's explanation: "Yes, Mrs. Lang, I know. You will probably see them together for the rest of this month. Your regular carrier is retiring. She is to be the new mail carrier on your route. I don't think you have anything to worry about. She's his daughter."

It must have been a disappointing setback for Sybil. Even so, she knew the young newspaperman from the *Weekly Standard* would be calling on Saturday night. She would be able to tell the neighbors when he arrived, how long he stayed, if they left and when they returned. She was "less than surprised" one morning to see Riley's car still parked in Joyce's driveway. This would be a juicy bit of information, and Sybil was more than willing to share it.

Joyce delighted in giving Sybil something to talk about. She would stand in front of a thin shade with the lights on and embrace Riley. The silhouettes could easily be seen through the shades. "Let's pour a little gas on the fire and give that old biddy something to talk about, not that she needs it."

Saturday mornings at the newspaper office were spent melting lead from last week's newspaper and pouring it into molds called pigs. These would be fed into the Linotype the following week. It was a never ending cycle and, along with the sweeping and cleaning, it sometimes seemed to Riley to be an exercise in futility.

As his final chore of the week he would tend to the "livestock" as he called them. He sat in the chair by the Linotype and held Missy in his lap. "You're one fine cat. Are you going to be a good girl while I'm gone over the weekend?"

Missy purred and rubbed her head against his arm. Riley emptied another can of cat food into her bowl and poured a small amount of milk into another bowl. Missy was placed in the orange crate with her kittens. Riley would close the shop for the weekend, take his Saturday bath and drive to Beaver Valley to see what was happening in the county seat. He would meet Joyce when she finished work.

Saturday afternoons served as trades-day throughout most small towns in the southwest. Farmers and ranchers and their families came to town to trade and buy groceries but most of all to visit. Never one to miss an opportunity to campaign, the local sheriff could be found within the same block every Saturday afternoon. It is doubtful Arliff "AA" Aten missed anything that was happening in the county, from the birth of a grandchild at Courtney Flat to a ten-pound catfish taken from Red River. AA and Chief Deputy Lawrence Bailey were in the midst of a conversation with Myron Proctor and Preacher Smith when Riley joined in.

"What's goin' on down your way, Riley?"

"Not a lot Sheriff. I guess the big news is that Missy dominoed."

"Missy?"

"Yeah, the cat that came to the newspaper a month or so ago. We have four new additions. I got her in an orange crate in the shop. I guess you'll be wantin' one of them when they're weaned?"

"Not hardly. Maybe you could talk Lawrence into takin' one of them."

"What's been happening at the sheriff's office?"

"We were just talking about that. Roy will be up Monday along with Truman from over at Ringling. We got some flyers from Dallas and I'll see you get one."

"Oh?"

"It seems they've got a serial killer on the loose. They're sending out flyers all over Texas and Oklahoma. This guy must really be a nut. He's killed four women, one in Dallas, one in Arlington, one in Fort Worth and one in Oklahoma City. They are pretty sure it's all done by the same man. I doubt anything like that will happen around here, but you never know. They have asked us to notify all the news media and get as much publicity on it as we can. We'll get a copy to the paper here in town and Truman can take a flyer to the Ringling paper."

"I wonder why they are sending it to rural areas like this?"

"I don't know. Probably because the murders have occurred in the Dallas and Oklahoma City area and our area is in between."

"Have the victims been sexually assaulted?"

"No, and that's one of the unusual things about it. The FBI psychologist has done a profile on these murders and he seems to think these are all related killings, but he doesn't have the foggiest idea as to why or what the reason is behind it. According to past histories, ninety-five percent of these type cases have also involved a sexual assault. But none of these cases do."

"We'll print it AA. What else?"

"The Department of Public Safety had a fatality north of Addington on the Cow Creek Bridge. Apparently some guy from Kansas went to sleep and hit the railing."

"I guess Roy can give me something on that Monday."

"Yes. He'll do that when he drops the flyer by."

"Thanks, AA."

"What are you doing in town? Come to pick up Joyce?"

"Yeah, we'll have dinner and take in the movie."

AA seldom missed a beat. Most people, excluding Sybil and the neighbors in Madden Grove, would hardly notice. But AA noticed.

# CHAPTER 2

Ben was in his usual position, sitting in his captain's chair by the cash register when Riley and Joyce entered the Casino Café. Saturday at dinnertime was a busy time in the Casino. Ben maintained small apartments above the café, and Beaver Valley was the overnight stop for railroaders between Fort Worth, Texas and El Reno, Oklahoma.

A newspaperman's mind is naturally inquisitive. For the most part, it's the way he makes his living. Riley thought of the earlier conversation with AA concerning the serial killings. One end of the rail terminal was at El Reno, just twenty miles from Oklahoma City, and the other end was Fort Worth. And Beaver Valley was the overnight stop for both the Fort Worth and El Reno turnarounds. Is it possible a railroader could be the killer? Perhaps he might even be in the Casino now.

"You seem preoccupied?"

"Not really, Joyce, just thinking."

"A penny for your thoughts."

"Oh, it's just a bit of information Sheriff Aten gave me today for next week's paper."

"Well? Is it a secret, or do I have to wait for next week's paper?"

"They've had some homicides in the Dallas and Oklahoma City area. They think it is a serial killer, so they want to get all the publicity they can on it. Really, that's about all I know until I get the flyer from Roy Evans next week."

Ben's menu included an excellent chicken fried steak, and Joyce and Riley took advantage.

"Well, what's it gonna be? The Royal is showing a Gene Autry shoot 'em up, and the Empress is featuring 'For the Love of Haley.' This is not Dallas, so I'm afraid the choices are somewhat limited.

I'm not sure what 'For the Love of Haley' is about, but I figured you would want to take in the Gene Autry show."

"You know it. That probably would have been my choice fifteen or twenty years ago, but Gene is a little quick on the trigger. Let's take in the other one."

"I can recall going to see Gene Autry and Roy Rogers when I was a kid. We had some old man who would rock back and forth in one of the folding chairs and hold his hands out like he was holding the reins when the horses were galloping. He would really get tied up in the action."

Popcorn and a Coke seemed to be a necessity, even though neither Riley nor Joyce was hungry after Ben's fare. They sat through the movie, and as they left Riley asked: "Well, what do you think?"

"I don't know. You laugh one minute and cry the next. I would rate it as 'different.'"

"I'll walk you to the car and follow you home."

"OK. When we get there we need to talk about something."

Riley had no idea what Joyce wanted to talk about, but he would find out when they arrived in Madden Grove. He couldn't imagine any problems between the two of them.

Following another car down the old 81 highway left a lot to be desired. White dust boiled up from the gravel road. Riley knew to stay far enough behind that he wouldn't risk flying pebbles and a cracked windshield.

Wonder of wonders, but Sybil had gone to bed. Most likely she had heard the cars coming and was peeking out her bedroom window. After all, Madden Grove was not the most active of communities. Joyce would often provide the only thing worthy of gossip. That the young newspaperman from Ryan would spend the night would surely dominate the conversation for the ensuing week. Joyce pressed on her horn as she turned in her driveway, just in case.

Riley chuckled as he opened his car door. "You're gonna give that old sister a heart attack one of these days."

"I just want to make sure she doesn't miss anything."

They kissed as Joyce flipped the porch light switch. "Come on in."

"Well, what's the big news, little lady?"

"John and Billie are selling the variety store and moving to Tulsa. Billie said the people who bought the store have a daughter in high school and she will help them part time, so it looks like I am out of a job. I'll work next week and that's it."

"What are you planning on doing?"

"I don't really know. I've got to work. That's for sure. I don't know of any jobs in Ryan or Beaver Valley. I have a cousin in Amarillo, and I called her last night. She is not married and has a good job. She told me she was sure I could find work up there. I don't know, Riley. I've been here in Madden Grove all my life, went to school here and married here. I guess you might say I'm a little tentative."

"I can understand that."

"I have enjoyed our relationship, and I know that for both of us it is one of friendship more than love. But that's all right. I found out in the marriage to Willie and my time with Fred that it is easier to get into a marriage than get out of one. Maybe people like you and me were never meant to be married."

"Well, you may be right about that. I've never been married, so I don't know. Maybe it's the uncertainty associated with it. The way we are, we can come and go as we see fit without any strings beyond those of friendship. That doesn't mean we wouldn't come to each other's aid, though."

Joyce grinned. "Yeah. A marriage sometimes can spoil a good friendship."

"I guess it was meant for most people, but then again…" Riley's thoughts trailed off. Aloud he said, "Are you going to Amarillo?"

"I don't see as I have much choice. But I don't want anyone to know about it just yet. I'll go there and see what I can find. If it works out, I'll come back and put this place up for sale. It's not really worth much, but it's all I have and I'll sure have no use for it in Amarillo."

"When are you planning on going?"

"I think I'll leave a week from tomorrow. I'm gonna slip out of town early before Miss Busy Body wakes up. She'll wonder what happened to me. That will give her and her cronies something to talk about for a while."

"I hate to see you go, but I understand."

"Like I said, I have enjoyed our relationship." Joyce laughed. "Our parting will be a little different that my last two."

It would be their last night together. It seems that all things, good or bad, had an ending. Sometimes a man didn't miss the water until the well ran dry, and Riley would think of Joyce in that vein as time passed. Joyce had been a good friend, but friendship and love were not always one in the same. Perhaps in some ways it was far better to like someone than to love someone.

Riley had toast and coffee with Joyce Sunday morning before he left for Ryan. They embraced on the porch.

"Best of luck, Joyce. I hope everything turns out well for you. Keep in touch and, send me your address. I'll put you on the mailing list so you can keep up with the news around here. Of course, this is going to be extra tough on Sybil. She won't have anything to gossip about with you gone."

"I would suspect she'll find something. Goodbye, my friend."

Riley turned as he opened his car door and raised his hand in response.

Sunday afternoon would be house cleaning time before his mother happened by to scold him for his "less than adequate" maintenance, but first he would stop by the newspaper to check on Missy and the rest of the livestock.

Missy's milk bowl was empty, but a trip to the print shop refrigerator would solve that problem. He poured Missy a bowl of milk and sat in the Linotype chair and watched as Missy was giving one of her kittens a bath. She came to the milk bowl and then to Riley's lap.

Riley's thoughts were of Joyce as he petted Missy. "I wonder what will become of her." He realized he was going to miss the good times they enjoyed together, perhaps more than he first thought.

Riley wasn't for sure which he dreaded the most, cleaning house, or listening to his mother if he didn't. One was just about as bad as the other, and nothing was left to do but clean.

It would be early to bed for Riley. But sleep didn't come easily. He kept wondering what was to become of Joyce. The night seemed to drag on forever. He tossed and turned half the night. Then, tired and bleary-eyed, he reached for the alarm at seven o'clock. It would be breakfast at Allen's Café, and the work-week would begin again.

"You look bushed this morning, Riley. Have a bad night?"

"Sort of. I just couldn't seem to get to sleep. What's been happening around here Mabel?"

"The usual—nothing."

Riley and Sara arrived at the newspaper office at the same time.

"How did the weekend go, Sara?"

"Pretty good, I guess. Brother Crampton announced in church that he would be retiring at the end of next month. He's been with us now for some twenty years, and he said it is time for him to step down."

"What's he planning on doing?"

"He said he and Mrs. Crampton will remain here, but they plan on doing a little traveling. He did say he would still work in the church and help the new pastor with revivals and whatever else he might need. He's been a good one, and we all hate to see him retire, but I guess there is a time for everyone."

"Yeah. I guess there is."

"Would you take the camera and see if you can get a picture of him along with him and Mrs. Crampton? I think it would make a nice story for the paper next week."

"Sure, I'll do that. Call him and see when we can get it done."

Riley went to the back office to check on the cats.

"Missy, you're gonna rub all the hair off your kittens if you don't quit bathing them. And I guess you want something to eat?"

The routine began once again. Sara opened the mail and brought the county agent's weekly letter along with a report from the governor's office and a release by the Oklahoma Department of Wildlife concerning the projected crappie population in state lakes. Riley started the Linotype, and the new week was underway.

Sara came to the back office. "I called Brother Crampton, and he said it would be fine if you wanted to take the picture this afternoon. He said around two o'clock."

"Okay."

Roy Evans arrived from the sheriff's office before eleven o'clock.

"Here's a copy of the flyer, Riley. Man, this is a strange one. They don't have a clue as to who this character is. All these homicides have taken place within a three week period."

"That is unusual."

"Yeah. And you read about cases where some nut kills prostitutes or some particular group of people, but in this case only one of these females was a prostitute. One was a secretary, one was a nurse and the other worked in a dry goods store. There's not a lot to go on. The most unusual thing is that none of the females had been sexually assaulted. I don't ever remember anything like this. I guess the only real clue they have is that this character must have yanked them out of their cars, because an abandoned vehicle was found near each of the bodies. The cars all belonged to the victims."

"That is strange. We'll put it on the front page, Roy. I can't imagine anything like that happening around here, but you never know. I guess this all happened at night?"

"As far as we know."

"And none of these females was with their husbands or some other man?"

"Apparently not."

"We'll tend to it."

"Thanks, Riley."

Riley had lunch with his mom and dad and took the camera with him.

# CHAPTER 3

The good Reverend Crampton and his wife were sitting in the swing when Riley arrived to take their picture.

"What's this I hear about you retiring, Reverend?"

"Well, Riley, there comes a time in every man's life. My faith is as strong as it ever was, but my stamina falls a little short. And, too, Madeline and I would like to do a little traveling while we are still able."

"Sara said you were planning on staying here when you retire."

"Yes. It's a good little community with a lot of good people. We've been here twenty-two years now, so it's home to us."

"I guess Sara has all the information. She sent me out to take the picture."

"Sara always has the information. If there is anything going on anywhere around here, she knows about it."

"Why don't we get your picture standing under the tree? That would make a good background."

"Fine."

"By the way, who is taking your place?"

"That I don't know. Like I said, Riley, this is a fine little community, but it is not on the list for most preachers. Most would rather go to a larger town. I'm afraid a lot of them don't know what they are missing. It may take a while to get someone in here, but we'll stay with it until someone comes."

"Okay. How about a big smile? And put your arm around her."

Riley took two shots. "How long have you been married?"

"Next May 4 will be forty-seven years. I don't know how the old gal has put up with me that long. But since she has, maybe she'll go the rest of the way."

"All right, Rev. Crampton. I think I got a couple of good shots. We'll get the film developed, and you'll see the story next week. I guess you'll let Sara know when your replacement will be here."

"That I will, Riley."

Reverend Crampton was right. Few preachers would want to come to such a small town. It sported one movie theater, three grocery stores, two cafes, a lumberyard, two banks, a pool hall, a few small businesses and a beer joint. The *Weekly Standard* was marginal at best and would have a difficult time surviving, except for a few loyal advertisers, its small subscription list and legal advertising required by state law.

But small towns had their blessings. The crime rate was virtually nonexistent. Red River was two miles from town and provided fishing and hunting for those so inclined. It would be ideal for anyone wanting to get away from the hustle and bustle of the big city.

The local drug store would send the film to Duncan to be developed. Together with Sara's coverage of the life and times of the Cramptons, it would make a nice front-page story for the following week.

Riley sat opposite Sara at an old manual typewriter and began his review of the flyer Roy Evans brought from the sheriff's office. He hardly considered it big time news for a rural newspaper catering to a farming and ranching community, but if AA wanted it covered, it would be. He could see the sheriff's reasoning given the location, halfway between Dallas and Oklahoma City. If the crimes were related, the perpetrator would surely have passed through here or the Ardmore area to the east.

Most area farmers and ranchers were more interested in the weather, the price of feed and the going rate per pound for cattle on the hoof than they were in the happenings in Italy, Australia, or some other foreign land. Not all would subscribe or read the *Daily Oklahoman* or the *Dallas Morning News,* both of which were sure to cover in great detail any serial murders within their area.

The traffic accident on the Cow Creek Bridge north of Addington would be more newsworthy to local residents, and Riley would be sure that was included in the upcoming edition.

"I guess it will be next week before we can put the Crampton's retirement story in the paper. I'll send the film off tomorrow, and we'll get it back probably Wednesday or Thursday. If you will go ahead and write the story, I'll set the type on it, and we'll get a jump ahead."

"I'll have it later in the day. I sure hate to see Rev. Crampton retire. He has been an excellent pastor. He and Mrs. Crampton are really great when it comes to caring for their church members. It is as though the members were all their children. I'm afraid we are going to have a difficult time replacing them."

"You never know, Sara. Who knows? You may get another Billy Graham in here."

Riley went to the back office and started the Linotype. He was not surprised when Missy jumped in his lap to demand a little attention.

"Listen, girl, I have work to do. You know you are a pest." Even so, Riley took time out to scratch behind her ears and fill the milk bowl. "Dang if you're not one spoiled cat."

Riley's mind was not on setting type. He wondered about Joyce. She would be leaving early Sunday morning for Amarillo. Would she be able to find a job? Amarillo was a long way from Madden Grove, and it would be quite an adjustment. But, as she said, she had to work. "Perhaps I'll call her about Wednesday night and see if there are any changes in her plans." Riley began to realize he was going to miss Joyce more than he thought.

The first four pages were on the press for the Wednesday night run. Riley remembered to call Joyce.

"What's new? Have you heard anything from Amarillo?"

"I talked to Cousin Beth Monday night. Believe it or not, her boyfriend works for the *Amarillo Daily Globe,* and he is some sort of a supervisor in the newsroom. I've got an appointment with him next Tuesday to see about a job."

Riley couldn't imagine Joyce working in the newsroom. "Doing what?"

Joyce laughed. "It's not as a reporter. They are in need of a proofreader. I ought to be able to do that pretty well. I had good grades in English."

"Well, that's great. Maybe one day they'll make a reporter out of you."

"Maybe so. I don't know. First thing I have to do is get the job. Beth seems to think I have a pretty good chance."

"I'm sure you will make a good impression."

"Thanks, Riley. I'm going to miss you. We had a lot of good times together." Joyce couldn't help but laugh. "I guess I will really be missed in Madden Grove. I don't know what Sybil is going to find to talk about when I'm gone."

"She's sure to find something." Riley couldn't help but think of Joyce's comment: "I'm going to miss you." Maybe there was more to the relationship than just friendship.

"When you get to Amarillo be sure to send me your address and phone number. I'll put you on the mailing list, and I'll be calling. By the way, I'm going to miss you, too."

"Thanks, Riley. I'll let you know how it goes as soon as I find out."

When Riley hung up, he felt very lonely. He picked up Missy and began to pet her. She purred as he scratched her neck. "You're a fine cat, Miss Missy." He placed her in her bed with the kittens and started the press run.

He worked later than usual that night, making sure the last run was ready early in the morning. Perhaps he would see if Roy Evans could get a little time off, and maybe the two of them could run a few trotlines in Red River. The weather had improved, and with spring just around the corner, perhaps the catfish would be biting. If he was fortunate enough to catch a few, he could prevail on his mother to cook them for supper. It was his father's favorite dish, catfish and hush puppies, along with a large slice of onion and maybe one of Mom's cherry pies.

Wednesday night required an extra scrubbing in the shower. Printer's ink seemed to find its way to every corner of his body. Riley called Roy before retiring.

"Can you get off work tomorrow?"

"I don't know. I'm pretty sure I can. I'll check with AA. What's up?"

"I thought we might run a few trotlines in Red River tomorrow. It's been a while since I've wet a hook, and besides, I need to talk."

"I'll call you in the morning at the newspaper office."

"Fine."

Riley had another difficult night. Instead of falling asleep, he tossed and turned, thinking of Joyce. He remembered his favorite dog, "Mr. Boots." He thought of how he always took the old dog for granted. He was always there, followed him to school every day and would meet him when school was out. And he thought of Joyce in the same manner, not as a dog, but as a loyal person he always took for granted. And now she would be moving to Amarillo. It would be quite an adjustment.

Morning came, and Riley had an early morning breakfast at the café.

"You look preoccupied, Riley. Something bothering you?"

"No, Mabel, just thinking about a friend." Riley wanted to change the subject. "What's for lunch today?"

"Chicken fried steak and stuffed bell peppers. The same thing it is every Thursday. Here, drink another cup of coffee."

The phone rang as Riley was placing forms on the printing press.

"Yeah, Riley. AA said that would be fine. What time?"

"How about one o'clock. I'll get the papers in the mail a little early and catch you after lunch."

"That'll work."

Riley met Roy at his home, and the two drove to the Red River.

"Gads, Roy. What happened to your arm?"

"Maurine Chastain."

"Maurine Chastain?"

"Yeah. Maurine Chastain. That's got to be one of the sorriest women anywhere. She was in Bailey's Bar and drunker than a waltzin' piss ant. She and Leslie Holmes got into it over something, and the fight was on. She hit Leslie with a beer bottle about the time I got there. It took me, Bailey and two others to get the handcuffs on her. She is absolutely the most foul-mouthed woman I ever saw. She talks worse than my old army sergeant, and I wouldn't be surprised if she couldn't whip him."

Riley laughed. "Man, she put a scar on you."

"Yeah. When I got her to the county jail it took me, Eddie and Howard to get her in the cell. When she gets her snoot full, she's a load." Roy chuckled. "Wasn't she your girlfriend when you were in high school?"

"Hell no."

The two men seined minnows from the shallows of the river and staked their trotlines above several drifts.

"You said you wanted to talk. What's on your mind, Riley?"

"It's Joyce. The variety store in Beaver Valley is being sold, and she's going to be out of a job at the end of this week. She has a cousin in Amarillo and she's going up there to see if she can find work. There's nothing around here."

"So?"

"So, I guess I'm gonna miss her, Roy. We've been good friends for a couple years now, and her leaving is bothering me more than I thought it would."

"Don't tell me you're in love?"

"I don't really know for sure. But I like the gal. We've had some good times together."

"How does she feel?"

"Well, she said she was going to miss me."

"Did you ever think about asking her to marry you?"

"Not until just here of late. Matter of fact, I never gave it much thought until I found out she was leaving."

"It's not too late, you know."

"I don't know, Roy. I just don't know. She's had one bad marriage and another bad relationship, and I'm not sure she would ever want to get married again."

"You'll never know unless you ask her."

"That's true. I am going to give it a little time and see how things go for her in Amarillo. By the way, she said she doesn't want it known around Madden Grove that she's leaving. It seems old lady Lang is the town gossip and she wants to give her something to wonder about."

"Yeah. I've had a few dealings with Sister Lang. She is one nosey dame."

"But about marriage, Roy. You're married."

"Yes. Phyllis and I have been married for seven years. Sure. We have a problem now and then but nothing major. I think that goes with marriage. No two people are going to agree all the time. It's a matter of give and take. I think she would rather I do something other than be a law enforcement officer, but that's the choice I made and I'm happy doing what I do. Most of the time, that is."

"Excluding Maurine Chastain?"

Roy shook his head. "You got that right."

"Well, I feel a little better talking about Joyce. She has an interview next Tuesday at the *Amarillo Daily Globe.* She hopes to go to work as a proofreader. Who knows? At least it's a start."

"Yeah. Maybe one day you can get her back here to work in your newspaper."

"It's a thought, maybe some time down the road."

The sun slowly went down as the two men ran their trotlines. Riley was lost in his own thoughts. It would be fish tomorrow night. Maybe his mom would bake one of her cherry pies.

# CHAPTER 4

It was going to be a lost weekend for Riley. What to do? The old print shop needed a new paint job. He wouldn't be spending any time with Joyce. Maybe after he did his Saturday morning chores sweeping and killing out last week's paper, along with the lead melting ritual that took place every Saturday, a paint job would give him something to do. It was certainly something that needed to be done.

Mac Steuver owned and operated the local lumberyard and had done so for thirty-five years. Mac would know exactly what Riley would need to do the job and Riley was more than happy to give one of his best advertisers his business. Sara would certainly be appreciative, as the front office hadn't had a coat of paint since Riley's father did the work some twenty years ago.

Mac had everything Riley needed, plus a little advice on how to do it. It would be a weekend of moving office furniture and cleaning. Mac recognized he wasn't dealing with Rembrandt when it came to painting, so he made sure Riley had plenty of drop cloths to cover the furniture, floor and anything else that might come in contact with paint Riley was sure to splatter.

The process went slowly, but between painting and petting Missy, Riley managed to use up the weekend and keep his mind occupied. He couldn't help but wonder if Joyce had made it to Amarillo. He would surely hear from her by the latter part of the week.

With the exception of the passing of Efram Johnstone and the retirement of Reverend Crampton, there was nothing unusual for this week's edition.

The weather was warming as spring made its entry. It was a good time of year, flowers in bloom, trees budding and the cold air of winter gone for another year. Spring didn't last too long in the

Red River valley. The dog days of summer always arrived sooner than later.

Thursday's paper featured the retirement of Rev. Crampton and the search for a replacement. It seemed the ministry had lost some of its allure and added to a declining church membership, filling the position would be a difficult task. The town's population had decreased six percent over the past ten years, and the church membership followed suit. Sara's husband was a church deacon, and she reported the search would begin in earnest the first of the month.

Friday's mail brought a postcard from Amarillo. Joyce had interviewed for the proofreader's job at the *Amarillo Daily Globe* and had been accepted. "I am working late evenings, getting off at one o'clock in the morning, as the paper goes to press around three o'clock. I will write more this weekend. Miss you."

"Miss you." That was good news, in a manner of speaking. Riley felt the same.

The local school board was pushing a bond issue, hoping to replace the grade school building that was nearly as old as the town. Three years had passed since the same issue was defeated by a substantial margin. This time the school board had an ally. The state fire marshal had threatened to condemn the building.

The board would advance a campaign sure to catch the eye of voters with something more than just a "we need a new building." Plumbing, gas lines, electric lines and a leaky roof were in a sorry state of repair. An explosion in the East Texas community of New London in years past had taken the lives of many school children. It was not beyond the realm of reason that such could be the fate of the old grammar school.

Riley attended the local school board meeting and would lend the support of the *Weekly Standard* to the school board's effort. Voters will generally support a school bond issue if the need is explained and justified, something the board failed to do three years ago. Secondary to the bond issue was the advertising support it would bring to the newspaper from local advertisers.

Riley would see that the issue was mentioned to some degree in each paper until the time of the election set for September. It would be hard to see how the issue could be defeated this time around, especially with the threat of closure by the state fire marshal.

Such was the life of a newspaperman in a small town. School bonds, obituaries, weddings, births, high school sporting events, farm and ranch news, the annual cake walk on Main Street and the Terral Watermelon Festival constituted the majority of the news. Riley sometimes wished for a change of pace. Some "news" could hardly be printed. The last big story in town was a year ago when the vice president of one of the banks ran off with the principal's wife—hardly something for the *Weekly Standard.*

April came the following week. Sara announced the church was "putting out feelers" in hopes of finding a new preacher. Riley received the letter Joyce had promised.

"Dear Riley:

"It has been a mad house trying to get adjusted to working nights. Beth works for a real estate agency, and it is not a very good arrangement, as she has to get up early and leave for work. And I try not to wake her up when I get home, but she is a light sleeper. She said she has a lead on an apartment not too far from the newspaper and I should know something on that later today. She says it is a pretty nice place and not too expensive.

"I like the work. One thing about it, we get to read all the news before anyone else. The paper covered the story about the serial killer in Dallas and Oklahoma City. I guess it is big news all over the two states.

"I am going to wait until I get settled in my own place before I put the house in Madden Grove up for sale. I don't know who would want it. It isn't worth much, but I have no use for it. When that happens, I'll try to get an extra day off and maybe we can visit. I'll send my new address and phone number when I get them.

"By the way, I really do miss you.

"Love, Joyce."

Love and marriage was something Riley wanted to approach with caution. He indeed had warm feelings for Joyce, but she had one bad marriage and another bad relationship. His heart told him one thing but his mind told him another. It might work out just fine, yet he still had doubts. He would give it time. Perhaps she was just lonely, not in love. If they both still missed each other the same after a few weeks, maybe he'd do something about it.

Riley's livestock had grown to the extent that he needed to put them on the market. He prepared the following ad for the ensuing issue:

"Nothing is free in life. The *Weekly Standard* is offering a special that is as close to free as free gets. To the first four new or renewal subscribers comes a bargain you won't want to miss. Four genuine purebred kittens sired by Sir Thomas the Alley King. Maternal lineage is of same high quality. Mother may be seen with her charges at the *Weekly Standard*. Father's whereabouts currently unknown. This is a one-time offering. First come, first serve. When they're gone, they're gone, hopefully."

Seven subscriptions drifted into the newspaper the following week. Four were from out of town and the remaining three gracefully declined the offer. Something had to be done. Perhaps a new approach was in order. The following week the newspaper contained this ad:

"I know all about you. I know your secrets. If you refuse to accept that which I have previously offered as 'free,' those secrets will be secret no more. I still have four beautiful, playful kittens to give away with any subscription. I'll even pay the taxes. Pick your kitten up at the *Weekly Standard,* please."

Joyce sent her new address and phone number. Riley called late the following morning.

"Well, how's the new job?"

"I like it just fine. It's taking a while to get adjusted to staying up that late, but everything else is going just fine. Amarillo is a big place compared to Madden Grove. The police are pretty good about being in our parking lot when we get off, so I feel a lot safer."

"Good. I've put you on the mailing list, so you should get a copy of this week's paper, probably Monday. Not much is going on around here. I painted the office and am diligently trying to give away four kittens. I may put a stamp on one of them and send it to you."

Joyce laughed. "I don't think the landlady would fade for that."

"Are you going to put your place up for sale?"

"I'm going to give it a couple weeks or so, and if all goes well I'll ask for some time off to come down. I guess I can turn it over to Mr. Brandon in Beaver Valley to see if he can sell it."

"Let me know. Maybe we can spend some time together."

"I'll do that. Hope to see you soon."

Sometimes when people are apart, they grow apart. Riley had seen many such relationships go sour, including Joyce's, that he was going to be cautious, perhaps more than he should. He could recall at least four of his classmates whose marriages had gone on the rocks.

"How many of them dang cats am I gonna have to take before you go to bumpin' your gums?" Wesley Sims laughed. "I read your ad. I don't know what you know about me or anybody else, but I don't need it in the paper."

"Sometimes a man has to do what he's has to do, Wes. I don't guess everybody knows about you slippin' on that fresh cow paddy and rolling in it."

"You wouldn't..."

"How many kittens do you need, Wes?"

"You're sorry. You know that, don't you? But serious, I have some mice in the barn and a good mouser might take care of that problem. I'll take that tiger striped one."

"They're free, Wes, but with your subscription renewal."

"Like I said, you're sorry. Why do you think I came in here in the first place?" Riley received a good-natured goose in the ribs as Wes handed him a check for the subscription. One down and three to go.

Roy Evans was in the newspaper office bright and early Tuesday morning.

"What brings you in here so early, Roy?"

"You remember the serial killings from a few weeks ago?"

"Yeah. I talked to Joyce in Amarillo. Apparently the news is all over the southwest. What's new?"

"Well, looks like we have another one. This time it's a lot closer to home. Saturday night the sheriff's office answered a call just outside the city limits of Bowie. Some citizen noticed a parked car just off a gravel road. There was a female in the car, dead. This time we may have a little more information."

"How's that?"

"Well, each one of these women has been strangled and they all have rope burns around their neck. And there always seems to be alcohol present in one form or another. This nut must get plastered and then goes hunting women. The autopsy report on all of them indicates they all had been drinking. They don't have the report on the last one as yet, but she's in the morgue in Dallas. Apparently this guy gets them drunk, rides out on a country road and then strangles them."

"I don't guess this one was sexually assaulted either."

"No, not as far as we know, and that's the odd part about it."

"It sounds to me like he has to get plastered to get his courage up. What else do they know about him? Are there any suspects?"

"No. If there are any, the people in Dallas and the FBI are not letting it out. I guess that's probably a good idea. If they make it public, this character is liable to pick up on it and change his tactics—not that we want another killing just to catch him."

"Bowie is only forty-five miles south of here. That's getting too close for comfort."

"Damn sure is. AA wants to be sure all the county newspapers give this one as much coverage as they can."

"How old was the last one?"

"Twenty-one. I don't think age seems to matter much to this nut. The victims range anywhere from twenty-one to forty-one. I wouldn't be surprised if the next one is fifteen or seventy. I've already been up to the high school and talked to the principal to make sure he gets the news out to his teachers and students."

"And they don't have the foggiest idea who this character is?"

"I'm sure they don't, or they would already have him under arrest. I'll tell you, Riley, this is a spooky one."

"Do they have any idea what time of day these murders are taking place?"

"They've all been found at night, so we assume they take place at night."

"I'll make sure we headline it in this coming issue. If there is anything else AA wants me to do, let me know."

"Thanks, Riley, we'll stay in touch."

Sara couldn't help but overhear the conversation. "You're not going to catch me out after dark, and if you do, my husband will be right alongside me."

"I would hope so. Why don't you call Rev. Crampton and the other pastors around town and let them help get the word out. I wish it were otherwise, but as you know not everyone takes the *Weekly Standard.*"

Riley wrote the following article for Thursday's paper:

SERIAL KILLER STRIKES IN MONTAGUE COUNTY

The Federal Bureau of Investigation in Dallas has announced another homicide, believed to have been committed by a serial killer. A rancher just outside the Bowie City limits found the victim. According to the Bureau, she had been strangled.

Evidence indicates the same method was used in other murders in the Dallas-Fort Worth and Oklahoma City areas in recent weeks. Special Agent Ramon Winters said alcohol was involved in each case and the women were apparently strangled with a small rope. He did not elaborate on any other evidence that might have been found during the investigations.

All victims were females between the ages of twenty-one and forty-one. The name of the latest victim is being withheld pending notification of next of kin.

Winters warned that the killer targets women alone at night, and that women who must be out late at night unaccompanied should use extreme caution. He asked for citizens to be alert and to report information concerning suspicious persons that might in any way be connected to these murders to the FBI office in Dallas or their local sheriff's office.

# CHAPTER 5

Desperate men will resort to desperate means to achieve their objectives. The *Weekly Standard's* back office had turned into a sanctuary for three little felines. Printer's ink, oil, grease, bits and pieces of paper and cats do not make a good mix. Plans one and two failed to get the desired results. A new and bolder approach was called for, and Riley would place plan number three into effect Friday evening.

His mother had told him many years ago that little boys loved dogs and little girls loved cats. Drawing from that bit of wisdom, Riley would attend the school carnival. With three playful, well-adjusted kittens in a box, what little girl could resist? He could hear it now. "Oh, Mommy, I want a kitten. Mr. Hughes said they are free. Mommy, can I have a kitten?"

It was a small wonder that horns were not protruding from Riley's head when he attended the school carnival. He hit the nail on the head.

"Mommy, can I have a kitten? Mr. Hughes has three of them and he said I could have one if I asked you."

"No, honey, you have dolls to play with."

"But I want a kitten."

And what "Mommy" could turn down such a plea.

Buster Henson got the same treatment. "Daddy, I want a kitten. Mommy said to ask you. Please, Daddy."

Buster had to relent. "Riley Hughes, a snake ought to bite you for this."

It had been a good carnival, a very good carnival. Riley ended up with an empty box, a few choice words from some parents and three very happy little girls.

Saturday morning found Riley doing the same thing he did every Saturday morning, killing out last week's paper and melting the lead for the ensuing edition. Roy Evans stopped by the newspaper office.

"Man, old lady Lang is about to go nuts trying to figure out what happened to Joyce. She called the office, and Peggy didn't know, so she wanted to talk to AA. He told her the variety store had sold and Joyce no longer worked there but he didn't know where she went. He called me and I knew she had gone to Amarillo so I guess the next time the old biddy calls AA can tell her. I have never seen such a nosey old woman."

Riley laughed. "And I doubt you ever will. Joyce used to do stuff just to give the old gal something to talk about. Now that she's gone to Amarillo, Sister Lang will be hard pressed for something to talk about."

"I have an idea she'll find something."

"What's new at the sheriff's office? Have you heard any more about the serial killer?"

"Only that the woman they found in Bowie had been drinking, just like the rest of them."

"I still find it hard to believe that none of them have been sexually assaulted."

"Yeah, but none of them have been. This guy must really have a vendetta. I wonder what's driving him. I imagine the FBI and the police in the Dallas and Oklahoma City areas are thinking the same thing."

"Well, let's hope they catch the sorry rascal before he commits another murder."

"What else is news around town?"

"Sara said they have a new preacher coming in tomorrow. She said he isn't permanent, at least not at this time. They really don't know much about him, other than the fact that he is not an ordained minister, sort of a 'jackleg' I guess. You know, one of those self-anointed types."

Sara had invited Riley to hear the new minister. Sara, always one to promote the church and any other news, suggested Riley bring the camera, and maybe they could get a picture and include it in a coming issue.

Rev. Crampton gave his usual welcome and offered a prayer for Sister Mabelene, who was in the county hospital. He gave a report on the past Wednesday night's prayer meeting prior to introducing the guest minister.

"Ladies and gentlemen, it gives me a great deal of pleasure to introduce Mr. Farley Branson, who comes to us from our neighbor to the south. Mr. Branson hails from a little town outside Corpus Christi, Texas. He became aware of our need for a new minister through his local church and came by for a visit. I convinced him to stay with us today and deliver our weekly message. Mr. Branson, welcome to our little church."

"Thank you, Rev. Crampton. Farley will do just fine. Ladies and gentlemen I must first tell you that I am not an ordained minister. My father is. He is certainly much more of a Bible scholar than I will ever be. Although I may not be as learned in the gospel as I would like, nonetheless it in no way lessens my belief in Jesus Christ, His Father and the hereafter.

"I would like to address the hereafter and man's perception of it and of God. We all know there is but one God, but there are as many perceptions of Him as there are believers in Him. I once heard it put this way by an old Indian: 'maybe my God and your God are the same God. We just worship Him in a different manner.'

"And I think that holds true. This is certainly not to compare the Almighty with any of us mortals, but we all perceive one individual different from another. The same is true in our perception of God.

"How do you perceive God? Is He sitting on a golden chair on the steps of a mansion, as might Julius Caesar? Are the streets in front of His mansion gold? Would it make any difference if they were concrete, asphalt or dirt? Is He floating in space wearing wings, as might one of His angels? Does He wear a robe, as pictured in many of the paintings that man's imagination has depicted Him down through the years?

"Just who is this Super Being we call God? Is He to be feared? It would seem to some that God is standing on the steps of hell waiting for you and me to make the least transgression so as to cast us into hell.

"No. I'll tell you who God is. He is 'love.' That's L-O-V-E. He is not One to be feared but One to be loved. He is a benevolent God. He is a caring God, ready and willing to forgive each of us of our sins. It has been said we are all sinners, and, with the exception of Jesus Christ, every man who has every walked the face of this earth is or has been.

"Each of you is familiar with the scripture 'man cannot live by bread alone.'" Farley grinned. "When I was a small boy I took that literally, but my dad was quick to point out the scripture wasn't talking about food. It means there are many more things we need, especially love, and there is no greater love than the love of God. If you love God, you worship God, and He will reward you, not just on this earth but forever in the hereafter.

"I wish to thank the good Rev. Crampton for inviting me to be with you today. I am not a minister. I am, as you are, a believer in the Almighty, and it is a privilege to meet with you today and worship Him. Thank you for having me."

Rev. Crampton took the podium and offered his thanks on behalf of the congregation to Farley Branson and gave a closing prayer. After the service Rev. Crampton and Farley Branson stood at the exit and shook hands with members of the church.

Riley had his camera with him. "Mr. Branson, I'm Riley Hughes with the *Weekly Standard,* our weekly paper. When a new minister comes to town, we like to do an article on him. I wonder if I might get a picture of you and Rev. Crampton together."

Farley Branson had a strange look on his face. "No, Mr. Hughes. I certainly appreciate it and if you want to do an article on it, that's fine, but I have an aversion to having my picture taken." And he laughed. "It's not that I am a criminal or fresh out of the penitentiary but, no offense meant, the article by itself will be fine."

Riley was caught off-guard. He thought it very strange that someone who made an appearance at a church wouldn't want his picture in the paper.

"Well, sir, if that's your wish, then we'll go with the article. Can you tell me if you are interested in becoming Rev. Crampton's replacement?"

"I guess 'yes' and 'no' would be the only answer I could give at this time. First of all, Mr. Hughes, I am not an ordained minister. Some people have even called me a 'jackleg,' or a 'wanna-be.' But I am not that. I doubt that my knowledge of the ministry is equal to the task."

"Of course, it isn't for me to decide, but I thought you did quite well."

"I thank you. But I have some other commitments just now. My father is getting on in years, and he and my mother can no longer manage by themselves. I am on my way to Kansas City to pick up my sister and take her back home to help me tend to them. I am hoping my sister can find work back home."

"What type of work are you in?"

Riley could detect Farley Branson was becoming uncomfortable with the questioning.

"I'm a vice-president for a bank."

"I see. Is there anything else you can tell us for the paper?"

"I'm afraid that's about it. I don't lead the most exciting life I guess. I work five days a week, go fishing when I can on Saturday and help out in the church on Sunday."

"Well, I appreciate the information. We'll get it in the paper and perhaps Sara can send you a copy."

"Thanks, Mr. Hughes."

Riley felt there was something about Farley Branson that didn't add up. He lay in bed Sunday night thinking about the interview. Why wouldn't Branson want his picture in the paper? There had to be a reason, but why? Apparently Rev. Crampton knew enough about the man to know that he was not a criminal. But if he had nothing to hide, why wouldn't he want his picture in the paper? It was something Riley would think about on a number of occasions over the next several months.

# CHAPTER 6

"Joyce called while you were out. She said she was called in early because one of the proofreaders had called in sick. She said to call her tomorrow afternoon early."

Riley had been to the county seat to pick up the county commissioner's proceedings. State law required they be published monthly, and the commissioners divided the work between the three county papers. It was the *Weekly Standard's* turn this week. Commissioner's proceedings, other required legal publications and want ads were a newspaper's greatest source of revenue.

"What did she have to say?"

"Nothing really, just to call her tomorrow." Sara added, "She did say she might get off in a couple weeks for an extra day or so and plans on coming down here to see about selling her house in Madden Grove. What's happening at the courthouse?"

"Not much. The only one they have in jail is Charlie Two Horses and the jail is home to him, more or less."

Riley thought he would see if Sara knew why Farley Branson didn't want his picture in the paper.

"Sara, what do you know about this Farley Branson?"

"Not much, really. My husband talked to Rev. Crampton about him. Apparently his father is fairly well known in church circles in South Texas But no one seems to know much about his son."

"I thought it very unusual that he didn't want his picture in the paper. Rev. Crampton was standing there when Branson told me he didn't want his picture taken. Did Rev. Crampton have anything to say about that?"

"Not that I know. What do you think about him?"

"Well, he seemed to be sincere, and I thought he made a good impression with the congregation, but I still can't understand why in the world he wouldn't let me take his picture."

"Did you ask him?"

"He just said he would rather not. I guess we'll go ahead and print the story, but it sure seems strange to me."

The weekly routine began again. Riley started the Linotype. It was a signal for Missy to rub against his leg. "Missy, you are one spoiled cat. I have work to do and, here you are buggin' me." Even so, Riley took a few minutes to scratch behind her ears.

The old Linotype moaned and groaned much like the press. Riley thought how nice it would be to have a new one, but the volume of business hardly justified such an investment. The machine was purchased new in 1919, just after World War I and was constantly requiring minor repairs. Riley figured that one day the old machine would crash and that would be the end of it.

Tuesday morning Riley made his rounds, picking up copy from his advertisers. After lunch he called Joyce.

"What's happening in Amarillo?"

"Just work. I enjoy the work, but I get a little bored sitting around the apartment. You'd think in a town this size there would be plenty to do, but I haven't found it. On my night off I did go with Beth to the movie. They have a little better choice up here than they do in Beaver Valley. What's new down there?"

"Old lady Lang is about to go nuts trying to figure out what happened to you. Roy said she called the sheriff's office. AA knew the variety store had sold and you didn't work there, but he didn't know you went to Amarillo. He called Roy to find out, so I guess the next time Sister Lang calls, AA can tell her."

Joyce laughed. "She is going to be in bad shape for something to talk about now."

"She'll find something. When do you think you are coming down here?"

"I haven't talked to the editor yet, but I thought maybe in a couple weeks. I hate to ask off no longer than I have been here, but I would like to get rid of the place in Madden Grove."

"What days are you off?"

"Right now it's Monday and Tuesday."

"I'd like to see you. I wish there was some way we could meet."

"That would be nice."

"I wonder. Why couldn't we meet in Childress, Texas? That's about half way. I think I could get some of the work done around here Saturday afternoon and leave out early Monday morning. Dad is still in good enough shape to operate the Linotype. I can get him to fill in Monday. Besides, he needs a little something to do now and then."

"That would be great. I noticed they had a Dairy Queen on the main drag through town. Why don't we meet there at eleven o'clock?"

"Fine. I'll see you then. If anything comes up in the meantime, give me a call." Riley would look forward to some time with Joyce. He was in need of a change in routine anyway.

The big Beaver Valley Rattlesnake Hunt would be underway the coming weekend. The hunt was in its second year and was sponsored by the local volunteer fire department. As was the case with virtually all volunteer fire departments, there was a pressing need for funds to buy new equipment and maintain what little they had. Prizes would be awarded for the most snakes, biggest snakes and a contest for a few brave souls who would dare to see who could stuff the most rattlesnakes in a gunnysack.

As Riley saw it, stuffing snakes in a gunnysack left a lot to be desired. He would leave the handling of rattlesnakes to those more daring. He loaded his camera and went with a local group to Ketchum Bluff on Red River, home to great numbers of the reptiles. Rocky caves and ravines provided excellent habitat for rattlesnakes.

Walking along a rocky bluff high above the river with camera in hand, waiting for someone to snag a rattlesnake from underneath a rock made Riley wonder why his father could not have been in the grocery or dry goods business, anything but the newspaper business. It seemed to Riley that being the publisher of a small weekly newspaper had many drawbacks but, then again, most every profession did. But taking pictures of rattlesnakes, fifty-year wedding anniversaries and watermelons at the annual Terral Watermelon Festival went with the territory.

And who would have the dubious honor of being this year's Rattlesnake Queen? The queen would be crowned on Sunday afternoon and this would require a trip to Beaver Valley to take pictures of the ceremony and prepare an article for the paper. He would be glad when Monday came so he could get away for a day or so and visit with Joyce.

The Rattlesnake Queen was picked from a group of happy young girls between the ages of six and ten. A smiling Cindy Webb from Addington was crowned "queen," and Riley and others took pictures of her holding a rattlesnake with its jaws sewed shut.

Ah, the life of a newspaperman.

Riley was up before daylight on Monday. He showered, shaved, packed some clothes for an overnight stay and began the drive to Childress. It would be a two and a half-hour drive, if all went well. He arrived in town a half-hour early, rented a motel room and had coffee at the Dairy Queen while he waited for Joyce to arrive.

Joyce arrived a half-hour later driving a late model car.

"Well, looks like you are moving up town with the new car."

"It's not new, just new to me. My old car was beginning to cost too much to keep it running, so I decided to trade it in. One of the girls at the newspaper is married to a guy who works for a dealership in Amarillo, and I bought this one from him."

"It looks nice. Are you hungry?"

"Yes."

"I rented a motel room. They have a café. It looks like the best place around here. Let's try it."

They went to the motel room first and unloaded their clothes.

"I've missed you, Joyce."

"I can say the same thing. We've had some good times together."

"Sure have. I remember Dad told me one time that absence makes the heart grow fonder. I think the old gent knew for which he spoke."

"I heard it put a different way. You never miss the water until the well runs dry."

Riley pulled Joyce to him and the two kissed passionately. It was a good feeling to once again have her in his arms. It seemed so natural. He felt at ease around Joyce, certainly more than any other female.

Joyce smiled. "I think we better go eat first."

Mid April was a nice time in North Texas and Southern Oklahoma. A cool breeze was in the offing, and clouds were building in the southwest. It was the rainy season, and the parched soil was in need of a good rain. After lunch Riley and Joyce sat by the swimming pool and watched a father and his three year-old son splash water on each other.

"I never saw a swimming pool until I was sixteen. I don't guess I would have ever learned to swim if it hadn't been for stock tanks. It is a wonder some of us didn't drown."

"We didn't have an Olympic pool at Madden Grove either. I guess there are some advantages to living in a bigger town, but I miss the country life. I hate to admit it, but I even miss old lady Lang and her constant gossiping. I guess when you've been raised in a small place you will have a hard time adjusting to a big city. I know Amarillo isn't Dallas or New York City, but it is a far cry from Madden Grove."

"Do you ever think about coming back home?"

"Oh, sure. It's just that there are no jobs. There is no one left in my graduating class that still lives in Madden Grove. Of course we only had twelve seniors. I think one of them is living in Beaver Valley, one in Wichita Falls, two in Oklahoma City and a few around the Dallas area. There is just nothing around there to make a living."

"Yeah, I know. I guess I am making a living with the *Weekly Standard,* but it sure isn't much more than that. If it wasn't for a few loyal advertisers, legal advertising and what other little dab I can pick up, it would be a tough go. And the sad part is, the equipment is getting old, and it's a constant battle just keeping it running. I don't know. There is no way I can buy a new Linotype.

I may check out some of the trade journals and see if I can find a newer one than I have. Some of the big dailies can afford new ones, so maybe I can pick up one from them."

They visited by the pool for a couple hours and the clouds continued to build. A few sprinkles came and they went to the room.

"I'm hoping one day that you will come back home. I know it is a difficult time for you. Frankly, Joyce, I don't know how much longer I am going to remain in the newspaper business, at least as a publisher-owner. I enjoy the work for the most part, but it's not too rewarding. I may work it a few more years and then put it on the market."

"Golly, Riley, it's been in your family for years."

"I know that, and that is the hard part. I'm afraid Dad would really be hurt if I sold it. It was his entire life's work, and he has it in his mind that it will also be mine. Perhaps it will, but I sometimes wish I was doing something else. You have to do certain things on time, or you won't get the paper out. It ties you down."

"I would think most jobs do. It's just the way life is, Riley. I suppose there are some that have inherited big fortunes, but you and I aren't one of them. If we don't work, we don't eat."

"Unfortunately you are right. But I am going to see how it goes over the next year or so."

Thunder and lightning increased, and the little West Texas town of Childress was treated with a drenching rain. Riley gazed out the window as a heavy rain pelted the swimming pool. He closed the blinds.

Joyce came from the bathroom and pulled back the covers and they undressed for bed. Riley pulled her to him and they made love. It was good to feel the warmth of her body and she responded. It was something they both had missed. It was a natural thing, and one that should not be denied.

They lay in the bed and snuggled. Joyce began to laugh.

"What's so funny?"

"I was just thinking about Sister Lang. If she could see us now it would give her something to talk about for a month."

"I would imagine."

They talked about Madden Grove, Ryan, and Beaver Valley and of things and people back home.

"I had a funny thing happen a week ago Sunday."

"How's that?"

"Well, Sara's church is looking for a new pastor. Rev. Crampton is retiring, or is trying to retire, if they can find a replacement. A fellow named Farley Branson was the guest speaker at the church. I attended so as to get a picture and do a story for the paper. This guy was pretty good, but he's not an ordained minister, sort of a jackleg, self-ordained type. He said his father is a full-time preacher in the Corpus Christi area.

"Anyway, after the service, he and Rev. Crampton were at the door to greet the congregation on their way out. I had my camera and was going to take a picture of him for the coming issue. He asked that I not take any pictures. He said the story would be fine, but no picture.

"The more I thought about this, the stranger it became. Rev. Crampton had to have some knowledge of him, but he was standing there and never said anything. I can't imagine why he wouldn't want his picture taken. I never gave this part of it much thought until later, but I am thinking Rev. Crampton must know why. Guess it's no big deal, but it sure has me buffaloed."

"That is unusual. Most preachers welcome the publicity. Is he going to be the new preacher?"

"Again, I got a strange answer. He said 'yes' and 'no.' He said his father needed some help physically, and he was on his way to Kansas City to pick up his sister to help out. Branson said he is not a preacher, but the vice president of a bank in the Corpus Christi area. If that is so, then why would he say 'yes' on one hand and 'no' on the other, concerning the position in the church?"

"That is strange."

"Well, I guess we'll just take a back seat and see what happens. Sara didn't seem to know anything about it. So much for that. Do you have any idea when you will be coming back home?"

"I'm going to give it a couple more weeks. Like I said, I hate to ask for time off for longer than I have been there, but I think the boss will understand if I tell him I am going to put my place on the market. I still have a few things there that I would like to pick up, and I need to find a place to store a few other things I don't need in Amarillo but would like to keep."

"Dad has a good-sized outbuilding. I'm sure he wouldn't mind if you stored some things there. When you decide, I'll borrow Roy Evans' pickup and get him to help me move it."

"That would be great."

Lovemaking was once more in order. The two finally went to sleep around midnight.

Riley awoke the next morning with a cold washrag in his face. "Get up lazy bones. I'm hungry."

Riley pulled her in the bed and they embraced.

"I really enjoyed last night."

"Me, too. It should be more often."

"Perhaps one day it will."

The visit had been exceptionally good, and the breakfast was excellent. They embraced once more and went their separate ways. Riley knew the more they were apart, the more he wished they weren't. He had a lot to think about on his way home.

# CHAPTER 7

Martin Hughes was not surprised when Riley approached him on the condition of the equipment at the *Weekly Standard.*

"Yes, I know it's getting old. It's just like a human being. The older it gets, the more that can go wrong. I could tell the Linotype wasn't in as good a shape as it was the last time I worked on it."

"I'm not against work, but it takes twice as long to get the type set as it would if the machine was in better shape."

"What do you propose to do?"

"Well, that's what I wanted to talk to you about. I know we can't afford a new one. I was thinking I might be able to find one in one of the trade journals. There is an outfit in Kansas City that rebuilds them."

"Do you think there is enough business to justify buying one?"

"If we don't do something within the next year or so, we won't be able to get a paper out. I think a rebuilt one is fairly reasonable. I'd like to get another model 14. The magazines will be interchangeable. We can transfer the straight matter and six-point to the new machine. Perhaps we can pick up an 18 and 24-point font and put it on the old machine, since we won't be using it except for headlines and ads. It will work fine for that. That will reduce the amount of handset type also."

The elder Hughes laughed. "I remember when I first started in the business. We didn't have a Linotype. They were just beginning to make them and they showed up first in the big cities. It was really something when we got ours. I couldn't believe how much easier it was to set type, that is after I learned to run the thing."

"What I wanted was your thinking on this."

"It will take you some time to recover your investment but frankly Riley, I don't see as you have much choice. You can still get a lot of work out of the old one, but a newer one is sort of like an insurance policy. And I'm thinking you might be able to find one at a reasonable price."

"Then that's what I'll do."

Riley had previously thought about postponing the purchase of another Linotype until a later date. Why struggle with the one he had when he was planning on buying one anyway?

Riley called the company in Kansas City. Several machines were in stock. The price was a little more than he had anticipated, but the cost included shipping and installation. It would be delivered in three weeks.

Roy was in the café drinking coffee when Riley arrived Monday morning for breakfast.

"You're up mighty early for a night owl."

"Yeah, I suppose. Do you remember Pat Foster, the school teacher in Beaver Valley who disappeared sometime back? She was supposed to go to her parents' home in Guymon over the Christmas holidays and never showed up."

"Oh, yeah, who could forget that?"

"Well, they found her body. Mallory Henson was searching for a cow on his place and found her in a dry creek bed. She was half covered with leaves and brush."

"When did this happen?"

"Yesterday."

"Do they have any idea who killed her? Is it the work of the serial killer?"

"No. At least AA doesn't think so. They've sent the body to Oklahoma City for an autopsy. AA seems to think whoever killed her is a local. I don't know why he thinks that, but I guess it could well be. There wasn't a car involved in this one. I mean she wasn't found by a car and all the others have been."

"Had she been sexually assaulted?"

"We don't know that either. The autopsy report will probably be back in a few days. We'll know something about that when we get it."

"There is no way this could be the work of the serial killer?"

"I didn't say that. What I am saying is the circumstances surrounding this murder and the others are quite different in several respects, so one would be led to believe this one was committed by someone else."

"If the autopsy report comes in before I go to press, and if AA will let the information out, call me and let me know if she had been sexually assaulted. If so, that would seem to let the serial killer off the hook on this one. Damn, Roy, what's the matter with people? With all these murders, I'm beginning to think the world has gone nuts."

"Yeah, it sure seems that way at times. I'll let you know."

"By the way, Joyce is going to try to get down here in a couple weeks if she can get off. She plans on putting her place up for sale. She said there are a few things she plans on taking back to Amarillo with her. Some of the other stuff she wants to store. I talked to Dad and he said she could store it in his outbuilding. I was wondering if we could use your pickup to move the stuff."

"Sure, Riley. I'll be glad to help. Just let me know."

News of a burglary was big news in a small town but when the body of a school teacher in a neighboring town was discovered, it would be the talk of the town. He knew as a newspaperman that both he and Roy Evans would be besieged with a number of questions. The finding of Pat Foster's body on the Henson farm would be the lead story for Thursday's paper, and he would hold it to the last possible minute hoping for information from the autopsy report. If she had been sexually assaulted it would surely eliminate the serial killer as a suspect.

Rural America seldom faced the problems of the big cities. The only homicide Riley could recall in his lifetime in the county was the murder- suicide of the Henrys over a family squabble in Beaver Valley. Several years past, Fletcher Davis, a black man, committed suicide by hanging himself from a tree near Beaver Creek over the loss of a French woman he had met and loved in France during World War II.

The wheels in his mind were turning. "If AA believes the murderer of Pat Foster is local and the serial murderer has now killed his fifth victim, the last one being in Bowie, where will he strike next? And is it possible that the serial murderer also killed Pat Foster? AA doesn't think so, but he could be wrong. Who is the serial killer? Where does he live? What does he do to support himself? Is he married? And what about Farley Benson? His story doesn't make sense. 'Yes' and 'no' is his answer as to becoming the new preacher replacing Rev. Crampton. If he is vice-president of a bank in south Texas, why would he quit that to become the preacher in a small town? Maybe he has his reasons. Perhaps a few questions for Rev. Crampton might be in order."

When Riley arrived at the office Sara was on the phone with Melody Andrews. Melody's daughter was soon to be married, and it would be another big splash. Riley couldn't see how a weekly newspaper could operate without a female reporter gathering such news as weddings and other social events. He thought women surely lived in a different world. Men seem to have a different perspective. Riley knew that Melody would spend several hundred dollars on a wedding when the newlyweds would be much better off in the long run if the money was used to buy furniture and some of the other necessities. But such was the way with the fairer sex.

Riley sat across from Sara and began typing the lead story—the finding of the body of Pat Foster. Sara talked for half an hour. How anybody could talk that long about a wedding escaped Riley, but he was glad it was Sara instead of him. When she finally finished, Riley asked:

"Sara, I don't guess you have heard they found the body of Pat Foster?"

"Oh, my, no. She's the teacher who disappeared around Christmas isn't she?"

"Yes. Mallory Henson found her body on his farm. The sheriff doesn't think it has anything to do with the serial killer because there are quite a few differences. I was wondering, what do you know about this Farley Branson?"

"Nothing really. Why do you ask? Surely you don't think he had anything to do with the murders."

"I don't know that one way or the other, and I'm certainly not implying that he did. Has anyone at the church heard from him since he conducted the service?"

"Not that I know. You'd have to ask Rev. Crampton about that."

Riley scratched Missy behind the ears and started the Linotype and began his usual Monday ritual, setting type on articles from the county agent, governor's office and a gardening bulletin from Oklahoma State University. Sara would have her usual "Mr. and Mrs. So and So went Somewhere to see Somebody" briefs. He sometimes thought he might be as well off saving the old ones from the week before, as they seldom changed.

Riley would have lunch with his parents and pay a visit to Rev. Crampton. Maybe the good reverend could shed some light on Farley Branson.

Rev. Crampton was on his knees in his garden setting out tomato plants. "Well now Riley, to what do I owe the pleasure of this visit? Don't tell me Sara sent you out here to check up on me?"

Riley chuckled. "No Rev. Crampton. I just wanted a little information if you have it."

"Oh. Sara's already got the information on next Sunday's service."

"That's not what I wanted to talk about. What can you tell me about Farley Branson?"

Rev. Crampton looked surprised. "Not much, Riley. Why?"

"Well, I thought it sort of odd that he didn't want his picture in the paper, and I was wondering if you knew why."

"I guess he has his reasons. Some people are a little reserved about having their picture in the paper. I guess he is one of them."

"What about the answer he gave when I asked him if he planned on applying for the position with the church. He gave me a 'yes' and 'no' answer. Why would he do that?"

"Maybe he hadn't made up his mind. You remember he did say he was not an ordained minister."

"I understand that. He said his father was. Do you know his father?"

"No, Riley, I've never heard of him. All I know is what Farley said, that his father is a minister in a small town near Corpus Christi."

"I remember he said he is the vice-president of a bank. Why would the vice-president of a bank come to a small town like this, and if he is a vice-president, then why would he give me the 'yes' and 'no' answer when I asked him if he intended to try to come here as the minister?"

"Golly, Riley, you ask more questions than Sara. I guess there is a lot I don't know about Farley Branson. He seems like a real nice person, and he may not be a great Bible scholar, but he is fairly knowledgeable on the subject."

"It doesn't add up, Reverend. There's something about this Branson character. I just can't put my finger on it."

"What do you mean?"

"I get the impression that he is trying to hide something."

Rev. Crampton placed a tomato plant in the ground and covered it to the top. "I don't know, Riley, maybe he is. What makes you think that, and if he is trying to hide something, what do you think that might be?"

"That's the puzzle. I don't have the foggiest. I wouldn't go so far as to speculate that he had anything to do with the killings we have had in the Dallas and Oklahoma City areas along with the one in Bowie. By the way, Mallory Henson found the body of Pat Foster on his property. AA doesn't seem to think her murder is connected to the others."

"My Lord, Riley, surely you don't think Farley Branson has anything to do with the murders? Why in the world would something like that even cross your mind?"

"I don't know Rev. Crampton, just a thought."

"Riley, I'm an old man. I have been in the ministry for forty years now, and I think I can pretty well read people. I don't know. Farley may not be who he says he is, but if the Good Lord would forgive me, I'd bet a dollar to a donut that he is not the type of person who would have anything to do with that."

"Well, I respect your opinion. It's like I said, things just don't seem to add up. Surely one of these days we'll know."

"Maybe so, maybe so."

"I guess I better get back to work. When will the tomatoes be ready?"

Rev. Crampton grinned. "In a couple months. You stay out of my tomato patch, Riley Hughes."

On his way back to the office Riley felt the good reverend knew more than he was telling. That raised even more questions. If Rev. Crampton knew Farley Branson was someone other than who he said he was, why the big secret?

"Maybe I'm seeing something that isn't there."

# CHAPTER 8

The autopsy report from Oklahoma City on the body of Pat Foster had not arrived at the sheriff's office Thursday morning.

"I checked with AA. He said they are expecting it any time, but they haven't received it as yet. The only other news is that Sister Lang called again, and now she knows that Joyce is in Amarillo."

"Well, that's hardly newsworthy. Then again, I guess it is in Madden Grove. Thanks Roy. I'll go ahead with what we have. Maybe by this time next week we will have more than just the autopsy report. Does AA still think someone local is the murderer?"

"Yes, but I don't think he wants that printed. It is only a guess on his part. If I get any more information I'll call."

"Thanks, Roy."

The lead article in Thursday's *Weekly Standard:*

SCHOOL TEACHER'S BODY FOUND ON HENSON FARM

The body of second grade school teacher Pat Foster was found on the Mallory Henson farm approximately one hundred yards off Highway 70, five miles west of Beaver Valley. Henson had been searching for a cow and found the body in a dry creek bed. The body was half-covered with leaves and brush.

Foster had been missing since the Christmas holidays. She was last seen the Thursday before Christmas. She was due to arrive at her parents' home in Guymon on Christmas Eve but failed to show. The second grade teacher had been in Beaver Valley for the past two years.

According to Sheriff Arliff Aten, the body has been transported to the crime lab in Oklahoma City where an autopsy will be performed.

Local Deputy Sheriff Roy Evans said law enforcement authorities do not think the Foster killing is related to the serial killings recently in the Dallas-Fort Worth, Oklahoma City and Bowie areas.

The autopsy report will determine the cause of death and whether or not the victim had been sexually assaulted. Reports on the serial killings do not indicate signs of sexual assault.

"What in the world is happening down there? I noticed in the *Globe* where they found the body of Pat Foster." Joyce continued: "Do they have any idea who killed her?"

"No, but they don't think it's related to the serial killings."

"It seems like when I left town things really began to happen around there."

"Maybe you ought to come back and bring us some luck. When are you coming?"

"I talked to the editor yesterday. He said it would be fine, but I am going to have to wait a while. The mother of one of the girls is sick in Dalhart, and she's gone up there to see after her. He said I could have the time off when she gets back. I don't know when that will be."

"Dad said it would be fine if you wanted to store some stuff in his building, and Roy said he would be glad to help us move it."

"Great. I miss you and all the folk back home. I don't know how I would make it if it weren't for Beth. I even miss Sybil."

Riley laughed. "Well, she finally found out where you are. She called the sheriff's office and AA called Roy and asked him. Sybil called back later, so I'm sure she and her cronies are wondering what you are doing in Amarillo."

"She's a piece of work."

"I'll be glad when you can come back."

"Me, too. I'm looking forward to it."

"If it's going to be a while longer than you thought, maybe we could meet again at Childress."

"Sounds good to me. Let's stay in touch."

Riley eased the phone back on the hook. He sat silently staring at the wall as if it wasn't there. He would face another weekend with little to do after the usual Saturday kill out and melting of the lead.

Missy came from the back office. It seemed at times that she had a second sense of when she was needed. She rubbed against Riley's leg, and he picked her up and held her in his lap. "It's a lonely time, Miss Missy, a lonely time. Maybe one of these days we'll change all that. But I guess you might be a little lonely with all your kittens gone."

Saturday morning Riley was pouring the last of the lead in molds when Roy Evans stuck his head in the back office."

"What's going on back here?"

"The usual Saturday morning stuff, Roy. What's new?"

"We got the autopsy report back. Pat Foster had been strangled and sexually assaulted. There was no alcohol present."

"So I guess that lets out the serial killer?"

"Apparently so."

"What else?"

"Maurine has been at it again. She was up at Stiffy's beer joint in Addington. She got her snoot full and Stiffy finally had to run her off. She got to the intersection by the truck stop. She had been weaving all over the road, and McGruder and O'Neal stopped her. They had the same problem I had, but they finally got the handcuffs on her."

"She's a terror. I remember back in high school she was always into something. As I remember, she wasn't voted 'most likely to succeed.'"

"They filed DWI on her and impounded her car. I imagine Judge Harris will give her some time in the county jail for this one."

"How much time do you think she'll get?"

"Not much. Maybe a week or so. It depends on what the judge thinks. He could give her a lot more, but as far as I know, this is her first DWI, so he'll probably give her just enough to let her know she better not make it a habit."

Sara had complained several times about her antique office chair. Saturday afternoon would be a good time to go to Duncan to an office supply store and see what was available. The old chair was like the Linotype. It had seen better days. He would stop in Beaver Valley. Sheriff Aten would, no doubt, be in the same spot on Main Street, given that it was Saturday afternoon. Maybe the sheriff had more news on Pat Foster.

"No, nothing new, Riley. This is a tough one. I had to call her parents and I'm sure they suspected the worst. I think that is one of the hardest things I have ever had to do, tell them we found her body. She was only twenty-six with her whole life ahead of her. She was to be married this summer in Guymon."

"Do you have any idea who the killer might be?"

"No, not at this time."

AA did not confirm what Roy had said earlier, that AA thought it was someone local. Riley knew better than to push the matter.

"That's pretty sad."

"Yes it is."

"I don't guess you have heard any more about the murder in Bowie?"

"No."

"Do the FBI and the people in Dallas and Oklahoma City still think it is connected to their murders and the serial killer?"

"As far as I know. We haven't heard any additional information about it. If we do, Roy will let you know."

"I heard the state troopers arrested our town's favorite female and you have her in jail."

AA had a frown on his face. "Man, she's about as bad as it gets. She was ranting and raving when they brought her in. Every other word was a cuss word. You could hear her all over the courthouse. I'm glad the rest of the offices were closed. I don't imagine the ladies in the courthouse would want to hear that."

"Yeah, I know. She was in my class in high school. She was a terror even then."

"I'm hoping she doesn't start that when she comes before Judge Harris. He's liable to throw the book at her, and we'll have her on our hands for the Good Lord knows how long. When she gets out, see what you and Roy can do about keeping her in your own town."

"Yeah. Thanks AA. Well, I'm on my way to Duncan. Sara has been complaining about her office chair, so I'm going up to the office supply house and see what I can find."

AA had mentioned to Roy that he thought the killer was local. He had to have a reason to think that. Riley wondered what it was. The murder took place four months ago. If someone local killed Pat Foster, it would seem that some evidence would point to that conclusion. It would certainly appear that it was in no way connected to the serial killings.

Riley's thoughts drifted back to Joyce as he drove the short distance to Duncan. His warm feelings for her left him wondering why he had never felt this way about another female. It had been ten years since he graduated from high school, and while the opportunities were there, none seemed to have the appeal of Joyce. Would she grow lonely in Amarillo and find someone else? If she felt as strong about their relationship as he did, she would wait. If not, it was far better to find out now than after the fact. Riley wanted to make sure before he made his move. He thought about two opposite quotes: "He who hesitates is lost," and "haste makes waste." No less a dichotomy existed within his mind.

Duncan was a bustling town on Saturday afternoon. Parking was at a premium, and three trips around the block were required before Riley found a parking spot near the office supply house. Color was relatively unimportant. Nothing in the *Weekly Standard* office matched anyway. Lady Luck was in his favor, as the store was having a sale on office furniture. He selected a tan swivel chair he thought Sara would like.

Riley waited for the red light to change at the intersection. As he turned the corner, he caught sight of a familiar figure talking to another man. "It can't be him. He's supposed to be in Corpus Christi."

Riley drove around the block, but when he came back to the intersection the figure of Farley Branson had disappeared.

"I almost know for sure it was him. But what is he doing in Duncan? And whom was he talking to? Maybe it wasn't him after all. Maybe I'm just seeing things but it sure looked like him."

Driving back home, Riley gave thought to once again talking with Rev. Crampton and maybe even Roy, but he decided to let it be. If he continued to press the issue on Farley Branson, people might think he was beginning to slip a little. "I'll just lay behind the rock and see what happens. If he shows up again, I'll know he is up to something."

# CHAPTER 9

Curiosity prompted Riley to attend church the following day to see if anything had developed. Perhaps he might mention Farley Branson and see if Rev. Crampton had any comments. Or perhaps he might learn of some new developments in locating a new preacher and the opportunity might present itself to ask some questions.

How close was "almost positive" or "almost sure?" The only thing Riley could say was "I thought I saw Farley Branson on the streets of Duncan. Maybe I need glasses."

Rev. Crampton announced the church would have a week long revival starting in two weeks. The preacher would not be a candidate for the position; rather, he would be a senior at the university, completing his degree in theology. It would be a part of his degree requirement to work in a revival. Rev. Crampton noted that the young preacher planned on returning to his home state of Colorado after completing his degree.

The old preacher always brought a good message, but Riley could detect it was not as easy for him as it once was. After the sermon Rev. Crampton waddled to the exit to greet his flock.

"Well, Riley, it's good to see you again. You surely didn't come to check on my tomato plants?"

Riley smiled. "No, Reverend. I came to hear the sermon. Have you and the deacons met with any possible replacements?"

"No. Not yet. I'm thinking after the revival they will begin a search in earnest."

"I don't guess you have heard any more from Farley Branson?"

"No I haven't. As far as I know he's in the Corpus Christi area seeing about his father."

"I guess Sara will write the article on the revival."

"No doubt about it. Come back, Riley."

"Thanks, Reverend."

Riley was sure John Crampton would not lie. Farley Branson may be in Corpus Christi and he may not. And he might well be in Duncan, Oklahoma. But if so, why?

Monday morning found Sara sitting in her new chair with a smile on her face.

"Surprised, are you?"

"I should say so. This is great. I think that old chair came over with the Mayflower. Perhaps you ought to give it to the Chisholm Trail Museum as an antique."

"I have no idea where it came from. It's been here as long as I can remember."

"I appreciate the new chair. Thanks, Riley."

"You're more than welcome, Sara. Rev. Crampton says you have a revival starting in a couple weeks and then the search for a new pastor begins in earnest."

"Yes. We're hoping we'll be able to fill Rev. Crampton's position soon. I think he'll be sixty-nine next month. He's getting tired."

"I could see that in yesterday's sermon. He reminds me of my dad in a way. It got harder and harder for him to get the paper out, and he finally had to give it up. He can still set type, but lifting the forms and some of the other work has passed him by. I guess it's coming to all of us sooner or later."

"You are right about that. I've been giving it some thought myself. Maybe in another year or so I may join them. A lady doesn't like to talk about her age until she is old enough to brag about it. I haven't got there yet, but I am gaining on it. When I decide, I'll let you know well in advance."

"You do an excellent job, Sara, and I am not looking forward to that time but I think I can understand. Well, I guess I'll set type on what's on the hook. I'm going to the high school this afternoon and talk to Maurice Matthews. It will be graduation time in less than three weeks, and I need to get a little history on his seniors so we can have that ready for our graduation issue."

When Riley arrived at the high school, Coach Park was in the principal's office. "Come on in, Riley. Maybe you can shed a little light on this conversation."

"How's that Maurice?"

"We were discussing the Pat Foster case. Have you heard any more about that?"

"No, not really. AA seems to think it is not connected to the serial killings in the Dallas, Oklahoma City and Bowie areas."

"What makes him think those killings have all been done by the same person?"

"That's really not AA's opinion. That comes from the police in those cities and the FBI. Apparently they are not letting much out as far as clues go, but there must be something that would lead them to believe that. I did hear that all the victims had been drinking and were strangled with a rope."

"That one at Bowie is getting a little close to home. I have advised the faculty and students to spread the word. Probably nothing will happen here, but I don't think it would be a good idea for a female to be out at night alone, even around here."

"You are right about that."

"I know you didn't come up here to talk about that. What's on your mind Riley? You have some suggestions for Coach Park concerning our recent loss to Temple?"

"No. I think I'll leave the coaching to the coach. It's time to get ready for our graduation issue, and I need to get the usual briefs on your seniors—age, parents, sports, hobbies, if and where they intend to attend college and all that type of stuff."

"I'll get the secretary to gather all that for you. We'll have it ready before the end of the week."

"Thanks Maurice. And Coach, surely you're not going to let Ringling win tomorrow night?"

"We'll take 'em Riley. We'll take 'em."

Monday afternoon would be a time to call Joyce. Riley was thinking about the comment Sara made regarding her retirement. She said she would work a year or so. If the situation with Joyce continued to move in the right direction, maybe she could replace Sara when the time came.

"How is everything in Amarillo?"

"I thought it was going fine, but the other proofreader quit, and I don't know when the one in Dalhart is coming back to work. It looks like I have a full time job, at least for a while. The husband of the one that quit works for an oil company and is being transferred to Casper, Wyoming."

"That'll keep you out of trouble."

"I won't have to worry about what to do on my days off because I won't have any. The only other proofreader we have works on days and works in the ad section mostly. I guess I shouldn't complain. I can always use the extra money."

"I was hoping we could meet in Childress, but I guess that's out."

"At least for the time being. I'm sure they'll hire someone else as soon as they can, and maybe Wilma will be back from Dalhart. I was looking forward to another visit. If the editor can find someone, I'll at least get my days off and maybe we can meet then. When Wilma gets back I can get a few days off and see about putting my place up for sale."

"It might be well in one sense of the word. I am going to be extra busy for the next two weeks. It's graduation time, and we'll have four extra pages to print. I know a twelve-page paper doesn't sound like much when you work for the *Amarillo Daily Globe,* but when you have an old hand-fed press and can print only four pages at a time, it's a lot of extra work. I may be able to con Dad into setting some type. I'll be spending a lot of time on the streets trying to sell sponsorship for the seniors."

"Sounds like a busy time."

"Yeah, it is. I'm going to go to Terral and out to Irving and get the information on their graduating classes. It'll be a lot of extra work, but it happens only once a year. The other big push is the Christmas issue, and that usually requires sixteen pages."

"Maybe things will get back to normal around here, and I can come down the week after graduation. I'm anxious to get the house on the market, but that's not the only reason. That might be better than meeting in Childress."

"Yes, it would. We'll get your stuff moved into Dad's outbuilding while you are here."

"Great."

"The Linotype ought to be in soon. That should be a big help. I guess I'll let you go. I'll be calling, and if anything changes, let me know."

"I'll do it, and I miss you."

Three obituaries dominated the week's news. It was sad to say, but a majority of out-of-town subscribers who were former residents took the paper for that sole reason, to see who died.

Riley had an unusual number of letterheads, envelopes, business cards and statements for Friday's work. He managed to pick up the information on the graduating class and would begin selling sponsorship ads Monday morning. He would work Saturday to complete the job work and to kill out and melt the lead for the following week. Hopefully, the Linotype would be in sometime toward the end of the week.

Selling advertising could be trying at times but a majority of the businesses supported the local high schools, and Riley managed to get sponsorship for every senior. He made a trip to Terral and to the rural school of Irving to gather the same information on the senior class.

Tuesday morning Sara received a call from Kansas City, advising that the Linotype would be delivered Friday, and the company would have it operational that afternoon. When Riley heard the news, it was as though he was an expectant father, and the baby was due.

As promised, bright and early Friday the new machine arrived. The double doors were swung open and power equipment was used to set the machine in place. Riley's father arrived for the big event and insisted on setting the first galley of type.

"Beautiful. It's really beautiful."

Riley agreed it was a fine machine, but he hardly envisioned a Linotype as being "beautiful." It was as if the old man was a three-year-old playing with a new toy.

"You know this is our graduation issue, so there is plenty of type to set. Besides, I can use the extra help."

The old gent set type the rest of the afternoon as Riley went to the other Linotype and began preparing the sponsored ads. With his dad's help, Riley would be able to print the first four pages Sunday afternoon. The special issue called for additional copies, as they would be much in demand by parents and relatives of the graduates.

It had been a seven-day workweek. Riley was thankful that every week wasn't graduation week. Even so, the new Linotype and help from his father made the job much easier than the year before. But Monday was Monday, and he would make his rounds among the advertisers, the funeral home and the usual routine would begin again. Sara would be on the phone gathering the news from the churches, schools and the usual travel column.

Riley returned to the office at eleven o'clock.

"Roy Evans was in here looking for you."

"What's Roy got on his mind, a fishing trip to Red River?"

"No. He didn't say. He only said it was pretty important and that he would be back in touch before noon."

Riley retreated to the back office and began setting type on copy Sara had placed on the hook. Roy arrived before noon.

"What's up, Roy?"

"They've solved the Pat Foster murder. You'd never guess in a thousand years who killed her."

"I haven't the foggiest."

"It was Buster Phillips, the high school basketball coach."

"You gotta be kidding?"

"I wish I was, but apparently they have the evidence."

"How did they catch him?"

"You know Deputy Howard Roberts, don't you?"

"When I see him."

"When they found the body of Pat Foster, Howard found a cigarette lighter on the highway near where the body was dumped. It had the initials "JAP" on it."

"That could be anybody, even 'made in Japan'."

"Yeah, but there's more. Howard was in Snider's Grocery a day or so after Foster disappeared and Buster was in the store. He had been scratched up, and his arm was bandaged. He said he fell out of a tree. Not only that, but Howard had been assigned to watch the Foster home at night and managed to get a partial license plate on a car that passed by very slow. Buster's car had a matching plate."

"Gosh Roy, I can't believe Buster Phillips would kill anybody. Why in the world would he do that?"

"According to the information I got, it was a 'love' thing. Apparently it only went one way. They were saying at the office that she had planned on marrying her boy friend in Guymon this summer. I do know the crime lab in Oklahoma City got some latent fingerprints at the crime scene and they'll make a comparison with Buster's prints.

"I talked to Eddie, and he was with AA and Howard when they brought Buster in. Eddie said Buster broke down in the office. He was booked on a murder charge and is in jail."

"Hard to believe that Buster Phillips would do anything like that. I don't know him all that well, but I see him when we play Beaver Valley. Man, that's got to be the biggest news in this county ever. Maybe I ought to go up to the courthouse and see what else I can find out."

"I'm afraid you'll have a hard time getting much more information than I gave you. There are reporters all over the place. It's not every day a high school basketball coach commits murder. This will be picked up nationally. I imagine it will be in all the daily papers in the morning."

"You're probably right about that. I'll just wait and get a copy of the Dallas and Oklahoma City papers. I imagine Wichita Falls and Lawton will also cover it. I think what I'll do is see what they have to say about it. Maybe I'll visit with Coach Park and see what he has to say. I understand he and Buster were good friends."

"Anyway, I thought I'd pass it on. Rather you hear it from us than read it in the paper. You do read the paper don't you, Riley?"

Riley grinned. "Yeah, Roy. Every now and then I even read the *Weekly Standard*. Thanks for the information."

Riley shook his head, still finding it hard to believe that Buster Phillips was capable of killing anything, let alone another human being. He would read the morning papers. In the meantime, he would contact Coach Park.

One thing was for sure—the Pat Foster murder was not connected to the serial killings.

# CHAPTER 10

"I guess you've already heard the bad news."

"Yes I have." Allyn Park shrugged his shoulders. "Bad news always travels fast. I still can't believe it."

"I don't think anyone that knows or knows of Buster Phillips can believe it either."

Coach Park stared out the window. "I've known Buster ever since he came to Beaver Valley. I don't think you could find a more gentle soul than Buster."

"I hear he had a crush on Pat Foster."

"I don't know anything about that. My wife and I have visited in his home a number of times. We were certainly competitors when it came to sports, but we became very good personal friends. He has a couple of fine boys, and I know his wife has to be devastated."

"I would imagine."

"All I know about it is what I hear from the people at the school. A couple of them have called. I think they were as surprised as I am. As far as I know, Buster was always a straight shooter, loyal to his wife and family."

"I guess we'll never know what goes on in another man's mind. From what Roy tells me, the Foster woman had planned on marrying her boyfriend in Guymon this summer. You would assume she was planning on moving back there if that was the case. And if that is so, she surely had nothing going for Buster."

"Sometimes rejection can be a brutal thing. I guess we all have thoughts we shouldn't have at times. I would have thought Buster would have better control of his emotions."

"I don't know him that well. I have spoken to him a few times at the ball games, and he seems a likeable sort."

"Oh, he is. A great fellow. I just can't get over this. If someone would have told me Buster Phillips was capable of murder I was have said 'no way'."

"What do you think will happen to Buster's family?"

"I don't think they will stay in Beaver Valley. I know his wife's folks live in Arkansas. I wouldn't be surprised if she didn't take the boys and move back there."

"Sad."

"Yes it is. I don't know what's to become of Buster. This is a capital case. He could even get the death penalty."

"This is true. Well, Coach, I just wanted to get your feelings on this. You know him better than anyone around here."

"He was a good friend, Riley. It hurts when something like this happens. God only knows how all this will turn out. It's enough to make you sick."

"I'm sure it will be in all the daily papers in the southwest and probably in the nation. I talked to Roy, and he said the courthouse is full of news people from just about all the area dailies and from the national wire services. I guess we'll read about it in the morning papers."

With watering eyes Coach Park turned back toward the window. "Yes. I guess we will."

There was little time for Riley to dwell on the subject. He had four pages of the graduation issue printed and still had eight more to go. He would work late preparing the next four pages and print them Wednesday morning.

Tuesday morning Riley had breakfast at Allen's Café. He purchased a couple of the daily newspapers and found the article on the arrest of Buster Phillips glaring at him on the front page.

## High School Coach Accused of Murder

Beaver Valley, OK—Local high school coach James A. "Buster" Phillips is in the Jefferson County jail after having been charged with the murder of second grade teacher Pat Foster. Foster disappeared before Christmas. She was to visit her parents and fiancée in Guymon on Christmas Eve but never arrived.

Helen McMurtry, Foster's landlady, noticed the front door of the Foster home open and called the sheriff's office. Sheriff Arliff Aten said the house was in disarray, and foul play was suspected from the beginning. State crime lab specialists from Oklahoma City were called to the scene and discovered blood stains in the bedroom. Lab tests indicated two types of blood were present, O positive and O negative. Crime lab specialists were also able to secure latent fingerprints.

Sheriff Aten said Phillips became a suspect when Deputy Sheriff Howard Roberts found a cigarette lighter with the initials JAP beside the highway, where the body had been dragged into a dry creek bed. Roberts had seen Phillips at a local grocery store with a large scratch on his forearm and his arm bandaged a day or two after Foster disappeared. Roberts also was able to get a partial license plate number from a vehicle that passed slowly by the Foster home the day after she disappeared. Those numbers matched the plate numbers on a car belonging to Phillips.

A search warrant was issued, and a blood sample was taken from Phillips. It was typed as O negative. The pathology report indicated Foster as having O positive blood.

People in this small town near the Texas border find it hard to believe that Phillips could be involved. One of the most popular men in town, Phillips was the class sponsor of this year's graduating class, which will graduate this Friday. He has been at Beaver Valley High School the last eight years.

District attorney Mike Dennard said he would present the case to the grand jury, scheduled to meet early next month. Phillips is currently being held in the Jefferson County Jail.

Riley spent more time Tuesday discussing the murder case with his advertisers than he spent on their ads. Everyone wanted to know what he knew about the case. Most assumed because he owned the newspaper that a newspaperman should have all the facts. He knew Roy would get the same treatment.

Riley was back in the office at four o'clock and the phone rang. Sara answered.

"It's for you."

"What's going on down there? I just got here and the lead story in the *Globe* is the arrest of Buster Phillips."

"Yeah, Joyce. It's the biggest news ever in this county. I talked to Coach Park up at the high school, and he can hardly believe it. He and Buster were good friends. I read the story in the Dallas paper this morning, and I have a little information from Roy. I don't know that it's true, but word is that Buster was in love with her. I guess it was a one way avenue."

"Yes, but my gosh, did he have to kill her?"

"I have no idea what he was thinking, but it really has everyone in shock down here."

"He was married wasn't he?"

"Yes. He had a couple boys, both in school there in Beaver Valley."

"What's his wife going to do?"

"Coach Park seems to think she'll go back to Arkansas. Her parents live there."

"That's sad."

"Yes it is. Has the editor hired another proofreader yet?"

"No, but he's supposed to interview one early next week. Even if they hire her, it will be a week or so before I can get loose."

"I miss you. I wish it would be sooner, but I understand."

"I'm on company time, so I guess I better get back to work. If anything new develops, let me know."

"Okay. We'll talk later."

Riley sat at the Linotype. Missy came and he picked her up and began to pet her. He thought about Buster, and how tragic it must be for his wife and children.

Although it was hardly a love triangle, since Pat Foster apparently had no warm feelings for Buster, he recalled a love triangle of several years' back. This one involved the wife of the owner of local service station and an area farmer. The service station owner became suspicious and noticed the farmer's pickup in town. He waited for an hour, shut down his business and went home. He took his shotgun with him. The farmer's pickup was parked a door or two down from his house. He eased up on the porch and gently tried to open the door but it was locked.

He kicked the door open and found just what he suspected. The farmer had begged for his life, and the wife became hysterical. Somehow common sense prevailed. The farmer escaped with his life, but had not been seen back in town since. The last time Riley heard of the service station owner's wife, she had disappeared in the Houston area. The station owner had since closed his business and moved.

Riley thought such situations might be humorous to some, particularly if they were not one of the participants, but it was food for thought. He couldn't imagine such a situation ever occurring with Joyce. It brought him back to an early thought: "Am I being too cautious?"

Men did crazy things, and Buster Phillips was a classic example. It must have been a horrible experience to want her so badly when she didn't want him. Buster probably could think of nothing else, and when she rejected him, it was more than he could handle.

Riley thought of the bad marriages in his small town. He thought of several of his classmates who had divorced and gone their separate ways. Then he thought of the good marriages, his father and mother, of Roy and his wife and more. Perhaps his time would come, maybe sooner than later.

Day dreaming didn't get the job done. He flipped the switch on the Linotype. "Down you go Missy."

# CHAPTER 11

Riley was behind his weekly schedule. He worked well into the night setting type and making up ads for the second press run. He recalled in his formative years his father was sure that Riley was not gifted with an abundance of free time. At eight years old, Riley began working as a printer's devil, first sweeping the floors and picking up excess paper that was sure to accumulate.

As Riley grew older his father taught him the fine art of melting and pouring the lead into molds. Fine art it wasn't, but a hot job, sure to bring perspiration to its maximum, especially during the summer time. In his early teens he grew tall enough to feed the old hand fed press. He would print the first four pages on Wednesday night, and while he was in school Thursday, his father would print the other four.

Last but not least came the Linotype. It was the most delicate and complex piece of machinery in the shop. Martin Hughes was not a taskmaster, but he was particular about the Linotype, and it was not until his sophomore year in high school that Riley began the process of learning the machine. He was now strong enough to lift the heavy lead forms on and off the press.

It was eleven o'clock before Riley had the four pages on the press. He would print them Wednesday morning and start preparing the last four pages for Thursday morning.

Thursday afternoon after delivering the papers to the post office, Riley took twenty-five copies to the high school for the senior class.

"Here's a copy for each of your seniors, Maurice. There are a few extras for your file and the class sponsor. If the students or parents want additional copies, they can pick them up at the office."

"Thanks, Riley. I know the kids will appreciate it. It may not mean as much to them today as it will twenty or thirty years down the road. I still have a copy of the paper when I graduated. I must say, it is a might yellow with age, but it's important to me to look back and remember some of the old classmates. That's been a long time ago."

"I've been giving some thought to hiring a printer's devil. The job won't pay much, but it will be an opportunity for a young man to learn a trade. It will have to be a male, because there will be some rather heavy lifting to it. Do you have a student who might be interested?"

"Oh sure, Riley. There isn't much summer work around here, unless you want to go to Terral and lift watermelons out of the patch, and that is sure enough tough."

"I'd think one who would be a junior next year would be about right. That would give him two years working summers and part time during the school year, and he could learn enough to get a job when he went to college if that is what he chooses to do. Any recommendations?"

"Do you know Ruth Hayes?"

"Yes I do. She was in high school when I was in the second grade."

"Then you know her son, Roger?"

"Yes. Is he going to be a junior already?"

"Yes, he is, and I know he would be just what you're looking for. You will remember his father and mother divorced, and no telling where his dad is. Ruth is having it pretty tough, and if it wasn't for help from her brother, I don't think she would be able to buy groceries."

"Well, Maurice, he may be just what I am looking for, but this job isn't going to pay much. It's a golden opportunity, though, for a kid to learn a trade. I'll teach him the Linotype, and Linotype operators are always in demand. If he wants to go to college when he gets out of school, he can surely find a job."

"He's a sharp lad and a fine one."

"Send him down to the office tomorrow. If he wants to work, I have plenty of it. A printer's devil is a long way from a white collar job."

"I'll tell him."

"Thanks, Maurice."

It would be a "win-win" situation for both Riley and Roger. Riley would no longer have to sweep the floor, and Roger could learn the lead melting process in one simple session. Feeding the old hand fed newspaper press was a simple task, one that would be of little value in that all the university towns had daily newspapers with rotary presses. The Linotype would be the key for Roger's future employment.

Friday morning Riley had breakfast as usual at Allen's Café. Two small envelope and letterhead printing jobs awaited him, and Roger would be in for an interview in the afternoon. It was time to call Joyce.

"What is happening in Amarillo?"

"Well, I got some good news. It looks like the editor plans on hiring this week as he has a couple applications, and he said Wilma would be back to work in a couple days. Unfortunately, that isn't good news. Her mother passed away."

"Sorry to hear that."

"Yes, but I'll be able to get some time off, probably next Thursday. He said I wouldn't have to be back to work until the following Tuesday. That will give me Friday and Monday to see about putting my house on the market. Maybe we could move the stuff to your dad's place over the weekend."

"That'll be great. I'll see Roy about using his pickup. If he's not tied up in his job he can help. By the way, I am going to interview Roger Hayes this afternoon. He will be a high school junior next year, and I have decided to hire a printer's devil. Maybe I can get Roger to help with the moving."

"A printer's devil? You must be getting soft in your old age."

"Maybe so, but I've been sweeping this place out since I was eight years old and melting lead nearly as long. Besides, it will give a boy a chance to learn a trade, and he can work his way through college if that's what he chooses to do."

"I'm really looking forward to coming home and visiting all my old friends. I don't really know anyone except Beth and a couple girls at the newspaper. It will be even good to see Sybil. No doubt she will have a thousand questions."

"I'll be looking forward to your visit."

"Me, too. I miss all the people back home, and I especially miss you."

"I feel the same. Call me when you can. There's not much going on down here. Things will get back to normal pretty fast now that the high school graduation is over. I guess the next thing will be the cake walk downtown in a couple Saturdays." Riley laughed. "When a cake walk is a big event in town, you know there's not much going on around here."

"That's true, but a lot of people do a lot of visiting, and that's what it's all about. I'll call you next week."

"Okay. Talk to you then."

Riley almost slipped and said: "I love you." Maybe he did love her. Joyce seemed to have time on her hands away from the job and had given no indication she had met someone else. Even if she had, she wouldn't say. Riley thought about the little boy who missed the school bus. Sometimes a man waits until it is too late to make his move.

Riley sat in the front office with Missy in his lap. His thoughts were of Joyce as he gazed out the window. Maybe the time had come. She would be home before long, and maybe he would approach her on the subject of marriage.

"I guess you're hungry, Miss Missy. How about a bowl of milk?"

A soft "meow" was his answer as Riley went to the refrigerator and poured his feline friend a healthy bowl full. "That ought to hold you for a while."

Riley had not seen Roger Hayes in a year or so and hardly recognized him when he came to the office. He had grown considerably.

"Mr. Hughes, I'm Roger Hayes. Mr. Mathews at the high school said you might have a job for me."

"Yes I do, Roger. And it will be 'Riley', so drop the 'mister.' My dad is Mr. Hughes. How would you like to learn the printing trade? There is always a job for a printer."

"I think I'd like that."

"There are a couple things you need to know. First, Roger, the pay will not be much. Next, it is a dirty, hot job at times. It seems we are always in a mix of printer's ink, oil and graphite. I don't know of any other job where a man can get any dirtier. Maybe the oil field."

"I don't mind getting dirty, Mr. Hughes, uh, Riley."

"What are your plans after high school?"

"I want to go to college. Right now I am thinking about either Southeastern State over at Durant, or maybe the University of Oklahoma. I've also thought about Midwestern University over at Wichita Falls. But that's going to cost a lot more money than I have. I thought about going into the military after school and then to college on the GI bill."

"If you learn the printing trade, especially the Linotype, you should have no trouble finding a job. I take a trade journal, and there are always plenty of jobs for Linotype operators. The pay is above average, especially on the daily papers. You'll find their equipment is modern compared to what you will find around here. For example, the old press was built around the turn of the century. Daily papers usually have rotary presses that can print thousands of copies an hour. Here we print about twelve hundred and fifty copies a week. The big dailies can do in two minutes what it takes us a couple hours.

"Even so, you'll learn how to make up ads, operate the shell cast and the rest of it. We'll take it slow and you'll be able to do a lot of it in a short period of time. The key is the Linotype."

"I'd like to learn."

"Good. Show up here Monday morning at eight o'clock. You know Sara Ingram?"

"Yes."

"She works three days a week, Monday, Tuesday and Wednesday. She gathers all the society news, marriages, and such.

"Your hours will be eight to five during the summer time and I say 'more or less' in that respect. We usually have to work late Wednesday to get four pages printed. You can take off Saturday morning after you sweep and do the melting. However, that would also be a good time to practice on the Linotype.

"I print the second four pages on Thursday. Matter of fact, I can have you running the press next Wednesday. It doesn't take long to learn that.

"There is a lot of cleanup work to be done around here. I'm afraid I have let a little of that get away, so first thing every day is to clean house, sweep, pick up the trash and so on. You'll have a lot of idle time around here this summer, so I'll lock one of the Linotype keyboards and you can practice on it. The sooner you learn that, the better. Do you type?"

"I took it last semester."

"Good. You'll find a lot of difference between a manual typewriter and the Linotype. These machines have a soft touch and ninety different keys. Quite a difference, but it won't take you long to learn. Any questions, Roger?"

"No sir. I'll be here Monday at eight."

"Great. Here's a key to the front door. Sara is usually here at eight, but if you beat her here you can get in. I'll see you Monday."

"Yes sir."

Riley had little doubt that Roger was exactly what he was looking for in a printer's devil—a sharp lad with plenty of muscle.

But with Joyce coming back in a week, it was time to do some long range planning. Riley wasn't Mr. Scrooge, but he knew the old saying "two can live as cheaply as one" didn't hold water. The *Weekly Standard* provided a living for Riley, but there were few frills along the edges. If Joyce accepted his proposal, she would have to understand the financial limitations. Perhaps she could replace Sara when Sara retired. "Surely a man doesn't have to pay his wife a salary," he thought.

Riley had his usual breakfast at Allen's Café Monday morning and was the last to arrive at the office. Sara was already on the phone gathering the news—who went where over the weekend.

Roger had broom in hand and was giving the shop a much needed cleaning.

Sara finally was off the phone. "Jamie Smyers' daughter had her baby in Fort Worth yesterday. It was a seven pound, three ounce boy. They've named him Jade Ricky. Where they came up with that name escapes me. The kid will be looking for revenge when he grows up."

"I guess you noticed the new employee?"

"Roger Hayes? Sure, I know Roger. Ruth attends our church, and Roger is there most of the time. He's a good kid."

"He says he wants to learn the printing trade and work his way through college. By the way, how is the progress coming on a new preacher?"

Sara laughed. "Not so good. My husband tells me they thought they had a good one. As it turns out, he got run off from his last church."

"What did he do?"

"He broke one of the commandments."

"Oh?"

"He got caught in a motel with the church secretary. I don't think they were going over the church's finances or preparing for Sunday's sermon."

"With that kind of experience, he could preach on the subject with some firsthand experience."

"Maybe so, but it seems the deacons are pretty narrow about that sort of thing so I guess they'll keep on looking."

Riley went to the back office. "Pretty messy, isn't it?"

Roger grinned. "It won't be for long. I see you have a feline friend."

"That's Missy. She just showed up one day and has been here ever since. I keep milk in the refrigerator and there is cat food over by the paper cutter. She has a way of letting you know when she's hungry. One spoiled cat."

"What do you want me to do after I sweep?"

"On Monday I usually set type on such things as the county agent's report, anything we get out of the governor's office and whatever else Sara puts on the copy hook. Why don't you grab a chair and watch while I set the type. It will give you an idea of how the Linotype works. This afternoon I have an envelope job for the job press that I didn't get to last Saturday. I'll set that up, and you can print those. It won't take you long to learn that. The printing part is the easy part; it's getting it ready to print that entails the work. We'll get into that this afternoon.

"After you watch the typesetting today, I'll lock one of the keyboards and you can practice tomorrow."

Roger marveled at the lines of lead type that came from the Linotype and Riley knew Maurice had sent the right man for the job.

# CHAPTER 12

It was a good week. Roger was quick to learn, and after a few adjustments he had his timing down pat and was feeding the old lumbering press like a veteran.

"Next week I'm going to turn you loose on the Linotype. I'll stand by to help in case you have a problem. The main thing is to take it slow and not get in a hurry. Speed will come in time. We are not in any hurry around here, and the faster you try to go, the more mistakes you will make. When you do, Sara will mark the mistakes on the proof, and you'll have to set the line over. I can tell you something about that. When I first started I thought speed was important, but I spent more time making corrections than I did setting the type in the first place. Read each line before you send it in." Riley grinned. "You'll make enough mistakes doing your best not to. I should know."

Joyce would be in Thursday evening. After the press run Thursday morning, Riley began the kill out process and the melting of the lead. He wanted to spend as much time with Joyce as possible, and Thursday afternoon would be a good time for Roger to melt and pour the lead pigs for next week. It was easy to learn but hot and heavy. One lesson was all Roger needed.

Riley was waiting on the porch at Madden Grove. He could see the usual cloud of white dust rolling up from the gravel road as Joyce pulled in the driveway.

Sybil Lang was standing in her doorway across the street as Joyce came to the porch and she and Riley embraced.

"Gosh, it's good to get home. I have to tell you I like my job, but there's no place like home, especially after you've lived here all your life."

Riley held Joyce firmly, kissed her passionately and the kiss was returned. "I've missed you Joyce. I really have."

"I feel exactly the same, Riley."

"I guess you never know how much you think about someone until they are no longer with you."

Riley knew Sybil was taking it all in across the street, but that didn't seem to matter. He kissed Joyce again.

"I guess I'm going to have to confess Joyce. I think I love you."

"You think?"

"Well, no, dammit, I do."

Joyce laughed. "Well, you are a long time saying it. I've felt that way for quite some time but, I mean, after all, you are the male."

Riley could sense the piercing stare of Sybil from across the street.

"Why don't we step inside? I think we are center stage and drawing quite an audience."

Joyce unlocked the front door.

"Now, Miss Joyce, I have been thinking—"

"Surely not!"

"Listen. Sara is going to retire soon, and I am going to need someone to run the front office and gather the social news, weddings, sheriff's report and the like."

"So?"

"So I thought you might want to come back home and take the job."

"What does it pay?"

"Room and board."

"Riley, are you trying to tell me something?"

"Well, yes...I am"

"Is this a proposition or a proposal?"

"Don't they go hand in hand, so to speak?"

"Is it or isn't it?"

"Yes, dammit, it is. Will you marry me?"

"Most certainly, Mr. Hughes. But about this salary thing, a girl has to have something for her labor."

"Well, I'll throw in a free subscription to the *Weekly Standard*."

"Your generosity overwhelms me. Is that all?"

"Golly, I didn't know you were a gold digger. I'll sweeten the pot. The next time Missy has a litter of kittens I'll give you the pick of the litter. I'm telling you, girl, you've pushed me near the end of my limit. But I'll throw in free lessons on the Linotype."

"I guess all the sweet romance I want goes with this deal."

"You got it."

"Now that we have reached an accord on the issue of marriage, when do you propose this should take place?"

"Why not this coming weekend? We can get the license tomorrow and get married across the border in Henrietta."

"That's fine, but it makes for a very short honeymoon. I have to leave early Tuesday for Amarillo. I will need to give the editor a couple weeks notice.

"And there are a few other things. Where are we going to live? What about the stuff I need to store, and what about placing my house on the market?" Joyce grinned. "See what you've done with this proposal? It's gonna call for some changes in our plans."

"Why? You can still put your house on the market and move in with me. I need to live where I am, as the paper is there, not in Madden Grove. We can still store your furniture in dad's outbuilding. My place is sparsely furnished, to say the least, so there will be room for some of it. If my place is not to your liking, maybe we can find another after you sell your place."

"We may be forty years selling my place. I can't imagine a big demand for housing in Madden Grove."

"One way or the other, we can handle it."

Joyce laughed as she stepped into Riley's arms. "You know, it sounds like we are negotiating as opposed to getting married."

"Sometimes you can draw a parallel. This is gonna be a give and take marriage. You give, I take."

That resulted in a short jab in the ribs. "I can see you don't know much about marriage. Women may be the weaker sex, but remember, we have what you've been seeking."

They both laughed.

"Now that we have that settled, who's going to be the best man?"

"Roy Evans. He can do that between helping us move loads of furniture."

"How romantic you are!"

"And who will stand with you? Or whatever you call her, the maid of honor."

"I'll call Evelyn Howard up in Beaver Valley. She was my best friend in high school."

"Then it's settled. We can go up to the courthouse tomorrow and get the license, and while we are in Beaver Valley you can see about putting your house on the market. We can't stay here tonight. We can stay at my place. I need to stop on the way home and see about Missy. She puffs up like an old dog if you don't pay attention to her."

"I'll meet you at your place—or should I say 'our place.' But first I guess I'll go over and enlighten Sybil. If she's gonna gossip, I might as well give her some fodder. I'll also tell her that I am putting the place up for sale. Between that and our marriage she should have an ample supply for a week or so."

Riley stopped at the newspaper office. Missy came and sat in his lap.

"I dunno, Missy. It looks like I'm making the big step. What do you think? Am I doing the right thing?"

Missy purred as she rubbed her head against Riley's chin.

"I guess that settles it. If you approve, it has to be the right thing."

Riley made his way to the paper cutter and opened a fresh can of cat food and filled Missy's bowl with milk. "That ought to hold you for the rest of the day."

Sparsely furnished didn't miss it far. "You don't have anything in the extra bedroom but a couple of old chairs. Mine will fit in there nicely. I guess the main thing we will have to store is the refrigerator and my stove."

"Maybe we can sell them. I'll put an ad in the paper."

"How much is that going to cost me?"

"Well, it's fifteen cents a line, and it will take about four lines. Lemme see now. Four lines at fifteen cents a line is—"

"You may be sleeping on the floor tonight."

Riley laughed. "I don't think so." He pulled Joyce in his arms and kissed her. He looked into her eyes, eyes like wells. "I think this is going to work out just fine. I love you Joyce. I really do. I just wonder why I didn't see this before."

"Love seldom happens overnight, Riley. It takes time. It takes understanding and it takes getting used to each other. We'll make it just fine."

"I have no doubt about that. I have some sandwich meat in the refrigerator. We can make out on that tonight and catch breakfast at Allen's in the morning. I guess before we go to Beaver Valley we can stop by my folks and give them the news. Mom has been wondering if we were going to tie the knot. I sometimes think she has a little Sybil in her. I guess she should. She gathered the news around here for over thirty years."

"I may have to tell her you said that. She'll like being compared to Sybil."

"You wouldn't?"

"About that ad in the paper—how much did you say it is going to cost?"

"That's blackmail."

"So it is."

Mid June in the southwest could be uncomfortably warm, but as the sun began to disappear over the western horizon a cool breeze drifted through the house. A gentle rain began to fall as Riley opened the bedroom windows.

"It's a nice night, a very good night. It's good to have you back home. I missed you Joyce, much more than you know."

"It's good to be home, Riley."

"We'll have a good life. Maybe we can't live on silk stocking row, but we'll have enough. Most of all, we'll have each other."

"Yes we will." Joyce removed her blouse and slippers and stepped into Riley's arms. She kissed Riley and grinned. "It looks like we will be celebrating our honeymoon a little early."

# CHAPTER 13

Mabel brought two cups of coffee.

"Welcome home, stranger."

"Thanks, Mabel."

"How are things in Amarillo?"

"They were fine when I left them."

"Back home for a few days?"

"No. I'm back home from now on."

"Whatcha gonna do?"

"She's gonna marry me, Mabel."

"Well now, congratulations. When is the big event going to happen?"

"Tonight. We're going to the courthouse after breakfast to get the marriage license. We plan on getting married tonight in Henrietta."

"Then I better not slow things down. What's for breakfast?"

Pancakes and sausage made for a good breakfast.

"I guess we should stop by the office. I need to tell Roger what's happening. He can help us move this afternoon. I also need to call Roy. After all, we'll be using his pickup, and I'm sure he doesn't know he's been selected to be the best man tonight."

"What planning! You think of everything Riley. By the way, where's my ring?"

"Good grief. I forgot about that."

"So?"

"So when we get the license and see the real estate agent, I guess we better make a dash up to Duncan and buy a ring. I don't suppose you'd be satisfied with an 'o' ring we could pick up at the auto parts place in Beaver Valley? Or maybe I could find one in a Cracker-Jack box."

"I am overwhelmed with your generosity. But the answer is 'no.'"

"I can see you are gonna be a tough woman to please, but a ring it shall be. We'll go to Duncan. Already I can see I'm gonna be hen-pecked."

"Deservedly so. But I must have a ring. You don't want people to think we are living in sin, do you?"

Roger was sweeping when they arrived at the *Weekly Standard.*

"We're going to move Joyce's furniture from Madden Grove to my place and dad's outbuilding. We'll need a little help this afternoon. I'm going to borrow Roy's pickup and he can help also."

Riley called for Roy, but his wife said he was not there. "He knows you want the pickup, and he'll help when he gets back from Terral."

"I'm going to need him tonight also. Joyce and I are getting married in Henrietta, and I need him for the best man. He is a 'best man' isn't he?"

Phyllis Evans laughed. "I'm not so sure. His mother thinks he is. I'll tell him when he gets back from Terral."

"We're going to Beaver Valley to get the license, put her house at Madden Grove on the market and then go to Duncan. It'll probably be early this afternoon before we get home. I'll call."

"Okay. I'll tell Roy."

It was a short ten-mile drive to the clerk's office at the courthouse in Beaver Valley. Arliff Aten was at the counter.

"What brings you to town, Riley?"

"Business, Sheriff, big time business."

"How's that?"

"You know Joyce, don't you?"

"Ever since she was a toddler."

"We're getting married tonight, and we're here to make it official—get a license."

"Well, now, congratulations. I was wondering when this was going to happen. You two have been courting now for two or three years."

"She talked me into it."

Joyce's eyes narrowed. "Baloney."

"What's news in the sheriff's office?"

"I was just checking to see what's on the docket. We have a trial coming up on a burglar Bill Crowder caught in Snider's Grocery last month. But I guess the big news is Buster Phillips murder trial. It's also coming up next month."

"Man, that was a shocker. Who would have ever thought Buster would be capable of murder. I know the coach at Ryan was sure upset. He and Buster were good friends. I guess you never know. Has the district attorney indicated whether or not he is asking the death penalty?"

"No. He hasn't said. I really wouldn't want to speculate, but Buster was a very popular man in town. We'll just have to wait and see."

"I don't guess you've heard any more about the serial killer?"

"No we haven't. Like every other law enforcement agency between Dallas and Oklahoma City, we've put out all the information we have. There's no telling when that nut will strike again. That type usually doesn't stop until he's caught."

"Nothing else?"

"Not unless you consider old man Brenner's cows getting out again. This is the third time this year. One of these days someone is going to run over one of them. That's the news around here, Riley, so you can see things are slow, just like we like them."

Riley turned to Becky Stillwell. "Have you got an extra marriage license lying around anywhere, Becky? Joyce here has proposed, and I just didn't have the heart to say 'no.'"

"Yeah I bet. You gonna let him talk like that, Joyce?"

"He'll pay. I have a lifetime to get even."

Becky completed the papers and handed them to Riley. "Best wishes to both of you."

"Thanks."

"I guess we better go to the real estate office next."

Brandon Real Estate Agency, like all other business in Beaver Valley, was a small operation. Ruby Brandon sat behind her desk reading the *Daily Oklahoman*.

"What brings you to town, Riley?"

"Joyce and I are going to get married, and she wants to put her place in Madden Grove up for sale."

"That's the old Melbourne place isn't it, Joyce?"

"Yes. Grandpa built it sometime around 1903."

"What would you be asking for it?"

"I haven't any idea what it's worth."

"I have to tell you that Madden Grove property is not in great demand."

"That doesn't surprise me in the least."

"Don has gone fishing with a couple buddies this week. When he gets back we can get the place appraised and see what it's worth. When he gets that done, we can contract with you, and we'll place a for sale sign on the property and advertise it. We'll advertise it in the *Beaver Valley Democrat.*" Ruby hesitated. Then she laughed. "And, of course, the *Weekly Standard.*"

"That's fine. You can contact me either at Riley's home phone or at the *Weekly Standard.*"

Riley often gave the impression that he was as tight as bark on a tree, but his bark was worse than his bite. He would buy a nice ring for Joyce.

"I know this is a strange way of doing it, but things happened so fast, it's the only way. I know it's the custom to buy an engagement ring and then a wedding ring to be presented at the wedding. I know the ring should come as a surprise, to be seen by the bride at her wedding. One thing about it, you'll be satisfied with it since you will have veto power."

Joyce grinned. "I know, but a ring is only symbolic of our love, and I do love you, Riley."

"And I love you, Joyce. I just can't understand why it took me so long to recognize it."

"I think that's a good sign. Sometimes this so-called 'love at first sight' is more of a physical emotion than it is love. Some folks get biology and love mixed up."

"This is true. We'll enjoy each other. We may not have great wealth, but we'll make it just fine."

Duncan was not Oklahoma City or Dallas, but is supported two jewelry stores with an ample selection of watches, pennants, ear rings, wedding rings and any other item as may be in a major store. Riley selected a beautiful ring with Joyce's approval, and the two drove back to Ryan. Riley put the ring in his pocket.

"The next time you see it will be when Roy hands it to me to place on your finger."

"It's beautiful Riley. It really is."

Roger was practicing on a locked Linotype keyboard when Riley and Joyce arrived at the newspaper office.

"I guess the first thing is to see about Missy."

"No need for that." Roger grinned. "She's quite a bum. I've already taken care of that."

"I'll call Roy, and we'll meet you in Madden Grove. Roger can ride with us. If it takes more than two trips, we'll just have to get the rest later."

Late June in the Red River valley can be uncomfortably warm and this day was no exception.

"This ain't perspiration," said Roy. "This is sweat. Man, no telling what it's going to be in July and August."

The three men finally moved the refrigerator and stove into Martin Hughes' shed and a bedroom suite into Riley's home. Joyce moved several lamps, bedding and smaller items. There wasn't much left; most of it could be transported in a car.

"Evelyn said she would be here at seven."

"That will give us time for supper and a bath. Phyllis and I will meet you at your place, and we can all leave from there."

"That'll work Roy. See you at seven."

"Man, I could eat a fried possum. I can't remember when I was so hungry. Why don't we get a bite at Allen's, and then we can clean up?"

Joyce was ready. "Sounds good to me. It's been a busy day."

Riley grinned. "And there is a lot more to be done."

"Sounds like your biology is acting up again."

"This is our wedding day you know. And what do people do on their wedding day?"

"First things first, and the first thing you need to do, Mr. Hughes, is take a real cold shower. That should adjust your thinking—at least temporarily."

"After we eat."

Big Shawn O'Leary had been a cook at Allen's for thirteen years. When he saw Joyce and Riley enter the café he came from the kitchen.

"Mabel tells me you two are going to get married."

"That's right Shawn. Tonight, as a matter of fact."

Shawn laughed as he wiped his hands on a greasy apron. "You know, Joyce, you could have had me. I'm a much better cook than Riley is. Notice how thin he is? If he didn't stop in here now and then, he would waste away to nothing."

Joyce smiled. "You're probably right Shawn. But I plan on keeping him out of the kitchen. Maybe I can fatten him up a bit."

"You guys are bumping your gums, and I could eat a horse."

"We don't have horse on the menu today, Riley. How about chicken fried steak? That ought to go over good on a man's wedding day."

"Sounds good, Shawn. Bring it on."

As good as it was and as generous a helping as Shawn dished up, it wasn't enough for Riley. He chased it with a large piece of cherry pie.

"Let's head for the house. I'll have that shower, but it won't be a cold one. Roy, Phyllis and Evelyn will be along in about an hour."

"I assume you will wear something other than Levies."

"For this occasion, my dear, I am even going to wear a suit and tie. But do look closely. The next time you see me in a suit will be in Tom Smart's Funeral Home. And when they plant me, see that I am not wearing a tie. The damn thing will choke me to death."

"Sometimes, Riley, I think you have a morbid sense of humor."

"Better morbid than none," Riley said as he stepped into the shower.

By seven everyone had arrived. Riley handed the ring to Roy. "Lose this, and I'm in deep trouble."

"Fear not my friend. It's secure. By the way, who's going to perform this ceremony?"

"Surely there is someone in Henrietta who is authorized to perform weddings. They do have preachers down there, don't they?"

"If they don't, we can always use Andy Bradford. He's been justice of the peace there for twenty years."

Joyce interrupted. "I'll be married by the preacher."

And so it was. Roy didn't lose the ring, Riley didn't drop it when he put it on Joyce's finger and when they kissed the good preacher pronounced them man and wife.

It had been a day like no other. A marriage license, placing Joyce's house on the market, a trip to Duncan for a wedding ring, moving two loads of furniture and a wedding constituted a full day. But Riley and Joyce were now man and wife and were prepared to settle into the everyday life of a newspaper family.

# CHAPTER 14

Moving the remaining items from the house in Madden Grove and setting type Monday would hardly constitute the average honeymoon.

"While you are in Amarillo, I'll check with Dad. He can't lift the forms, but Roger can. I'll ask Dad to set the type and make up the paper. Roger can run the press so that should work out. I'm going to start Roger on the Linotype this week, but it will take a while before he is able to set much type. So, we'll have a week. Where would you like to go on a honeymoon? Childress or Amarillo?"

"You gotta be kidding. How about Lake City, Colorado? I hear it's really nice this time of the year. We can get away from this heat for a week. We had a series in the *Globe* on the area. The Lake Fork of the Gunnison River runs through town, and there is an old abandoned mining town on Henson Creek. Lake City is the only place in the United States where they had a trial for cannibalism. It's called the Packer Massacre. All his victims are buried there, that is, what was left of them."

"Sounds great to me. Maybe we could pack a lunch and have a picnic at the burial site."

"I sometimes think you have a demented sense of humor."

"In this business, you gotta have."

"I can check for reservations when I get back to Amarillo. The article mentioned a place called T Mountain that has cabins. Maybe we could stay there."

"We can leave on Friday and we won't have to be back until a week from Sunday. Go ahead and make the reservations. I imagine I'll be ready. The Terral Watermelon Festival is the next weekend, and I'll have to cover that. It's always hotter than the devil's den down there, so I'll welcome a cooler climate."

"You can pick me up in Amarillo. It's on the way. We can pick my stuff up at the apartment on our way back. We can leave my car in Amarillo. That way we'll have two cars, and I imagine with my clothes and a couple things I picked up we'll need the space."

"We'll handle it that way."

Riley Hughes fell short of America's greatest house cleaner, and Joyce spent two days dusting, washing, vacuuming and throwing away junk.

"Ye gads, Riley. Has your mother been over here lately? There's enough dust on the windowsills to start a garden."

"I never let Mom past the front room."

"That stands to reason. But I guess you're like a lot of other men. Housework doesn't seem to be your main forte."

Riley grinned. "How could you tell?"

"Listen closely, Mr. Hughes. I am cleaning this place top to bottom, and when we get back from Lake City, I'll expect it to be in the same shape I've left it." Joyce punched Riley in the ribs. "You got that?"

"Yes ma'am." Riley winked as he pulled Joyce on the couch and kissed her. "I see you're gonna be a mean momma. It sounds like the fairy god mother is gonna turn into the wicked witch of the north."

They both laughed as they wrestled on the couch.

"I love you, Riley."

"And I love you, Joyce. I am thinking we are going to make it just fine. We won't have the most, and we won't have the best, but if two people are happy with each other, very little else matters."

The weekend came and went faster than the two of them would have preferred. Monday Joyce would make the short trip to Beaver Valley and sign a contract on her house in Madden Grove.

"I can't imagine, but maybe someone wants to move to an out of the way place, and Madden Grove has to be on the top of the list."

A cheerful Sara greeted Riley Monday morning.

"Well, the news is out. I hear you and Joyce finally decided to tie the knot. I'd say it is about time."

"Yeah. She asked me, and I just didn't have the heart to refuse."

"You tell that around town and nobody will ever believe a word you say."

"I'm not sure they do any way."

"On another matter, Riley, I've been thinking about retiring within the year. Now that you have Joyce, maybe she could take my place when she gets back from Amarillo. My husband isn't in the best of health, and we'd like to do a little traveling while he is still able."

"I can understand that. Maybe you could stay on with her for a couple weeks when she gets back."

"I'll do that, and I'll still be a contributor."

"I sort of face your retirement with mixed emotions. You've been an excellent hand. I guess there comes a time for all of us to retire."

"Thanks, Riley. Well, so much for my retirement. I've got to call Elaine Griffin. She's ramrodding the school reunion set for the Labor Day weekend, so I know she'll want as much publicity as she can get."

"Yeah. And I've got to meet with the school board tonight to go over their plans for the proposed school bond issue for the new grade school. I had hoped to spend a little more time with Joyce before she goes back to Amarillo."

"You'll have a lifetime for that."

"I suppose you're right. Well, I'm going to start Roger on the Linotype today. I can remember when Dad started with me. I hope I have the old man's patience. Seems I could screw things up worse than Hogan's goat at times, but Dad was always there to fix whatever went wrong."

Riley entered the back office to find Roger practicing on a locked keyboard. Missy was rubbing against Roger's leg, anxious for the attention she didn't get over the weekend.

"We'll unlock the keyboard and you can set your first line of type today. You can take the governor's weekly report. None too exciting, but it is a weekly feature. I'll watch for a while, and then

I'll work on the other machine. Remember that slow and easy does it. This is not the *Dallas Morning News* or the *Daily Oklahoman.*"

Riley sat in a chair beside Roger and held Missy in his lap. It was a slow process, but it wouldn't be long before Roger could set type as well as anyone.

Joyce would be home for lunch, and he would advise her of her new job as society editor.

"I've never written a single story. Maybe I can't do it."

"Sara will stay with you a couple weeks. You'll do just fine. You may have to develop a little more Sybil than you have. A society editor has to be a little nosey. That's why only women are society editors," Riley said as he took a punch in the rib cage. "We don't have to worry about national news, foreign news, the stock market report or anything else like that. The big dailies handle that. Our readers are interested in who is getting married, who visiting whom, local high school activities and sports and such.

"We have to get involved in a lot of community projects, such as the school board meetings, which I have to attend tonight. Then there is the annual school carnival, the cakewalk and the Terral Watermelon Festival, which I'll get a dose of next weekend while you are in Amarillo. Rarely do we have any local news that attracts statewide or national attention, but the arrest and trial of Buster Phillips up at Beaver Valley will be one I'll have to make."

"Well, I'll take that up when we get back from Lake City. I'll have to leave early in the morning to get there by work time."

Back at the shop Roger had finished his first galley of type. Riley laughed when Sara brought back the proof with a dozen errors plainly marked."

"Gee, I thought I would do better than that."

"That's what I thought the first time I set type. You'll just have to make the corrections. The more corrections you have to make, the less you will want to make, and that in itself will force your improvement. I ought to know. My first proof looked like a chicken had tracked all over it."

Roger shook his head. "I'll sure have to get better than this."

"Don't worry. You will."

Riley's night at the school board meeting lasted longer than he had hoped. It was time for the annual review of the faculty, the superintendent's report and a presentation on the proposed bond issue for the grade school. It was nine-thirty before Riley arrived home.

"Gee, I wish we had more time together before you went back to Amarillo. I guess it's like Sara said, we'll have plenty of time together in a couple weeks."

"I would think so, since we'll not only be living together but working together."

Light rain fell as Riley opened the window. A soft breeze drifted through the bedroom. "Rain smells good. I like it when it rains. It seems to clear the air. It is a good night for people in love." And love they did.

"Yes, and we'll sleep well tonight." And they did that, too.

Riley awoke to the smell of freshly brewed coffee.

"Time to get up. It's toast and coffee this morning. I've got to hit the road. It's five hours to Amarillo."

Breakfast was short. "I'm on my way. I'll call you at the office when I get there."

"I'll be looking forward to our trip to Lake City. In the meantime, I'll give you a detailed report on the Terral Watermelon Festival this coming weekend."

"Gee thanks. Maybe you can mail me a copy of the paper or bring one with you when you come." Joyce frowned. "I guess if three murders, four robberies and a sexual assault occur, they'll all take back page to the Watermelon Festival."

"You got it."

As Joyce left for Amarillo Riley thought how nice it would be to spend a week in the mountains, away from the work-a-day world. It would be his first vacation in memory and something he hoped could be arranged on a frequent basis.

Riley joked about the Terral Watermelon Festival, in large part because of his dislike for watermelons. Even so, it was a boost for Terral and the surrounding area. Red River was only a stone's throw from the little community, and the sandy soil produced some of the best melons to be shipped throughout the country.

The week finally passed and, with camera in hand, Riley made the short trip to Terral. Sheriff Aten and Roy Evans were sure to be there, mingling among the crowd, as would state Representative Malcolm Barrow from Duncan. It was as much a county "get-together" as it was a promotion of watermelons.

Riley had often expressed his dislike for the taste of watermelon, and Roy couldn't help but chide him. "I guess you'll pig out on melon again this year."

"I'd as soon eat a gourd. But I guess I'm in a definite minority here."

"Seems you are," Roy said as he sprinkled a slice of cold melon with salt. "Man, you don't know what you're missing."

"Where's AA?"

"He's around here somewhere. Last I saw of him, he was talking to the good Reverend Crampton."

"Well, I guess I'd better get a shot or two for next week's paper."

Riley mingled with the crowd on his way to the grandstand. It would be time for the crowning of the festival queen—little nine-year-old Melody Mullanax of Terral.

As he was moving to make a third shot of Melody, he noticed a familiar figure in the crowd, none other than Farley Branson. What is Farley Branson doing at the Terral Watermelon Festival? Surely he didn't drive all the way from south Texas just to eat watermelon. Maybe he was going to take the pulpit for Reverend Crampton Sunday.

Riley Hughes eased his way through the crowd to a table where Branson and several others were getting their fill of cold watermelon.

"Well, Mr. Branson. What brings you to Terral? Surely you didn't drive all the way up here from the valley just to eat watermelon?"

Farley Branson looked up from his slice of melon. "You're right about that, Mr. Editor. I thought I would indulge. These are the best melons anywhere."

"Did you come to fill in for Rev. Crampton tomorrow?"

"No. But I did come to visit with him. He's a good old gent. Actually, I'm on my way to visit a cousin in Winfield, Kansas and then on to Kansas City to help my sister wind up some of her business. She's moving back with me to help take care of Dad."

"How did you meet Reverend Crampton?"

Farley Branson looked at Riley as if to say "You ask too many questions." He took another bite of melon. "As I told you before, my Dad is a minister. He keeps up with what's happening in the churches. That's his life. Somewhere in the past he knew of Rev. Crampton and found out that he was retiring. That's how I got into the act. Dad asked me to visit with him when I came this way. Rev. Crampton asked me to say a few words at his church that Sunday. So I did."

"And you did a good job. Did you ever think about following in your father's footsteps and joining the ministry?"

"In my younger days, yes. That's what Dad wanted me to do. But sometimes things seem to take a turn, and I had an opportunity to go into the banking business and I enjoyed it. So . . ." and Branson shrugged his shoulders.

"Well, good to see you again. Hope your trip goes well."

"Thanks."

Riley retreated to the grandstand to be greeted by the happy and proud parents of the festival queen. One more picture of Melody sandwiched between her parents, and the festival was laid to rest for another year.

Something about Farley Branson's story didn't ring true. Maybe Riley was letting his imagination run away with him, but it was like putting square pegs in round holes. A bank executive? It just didn't seem to fit Farley Branson. But if not that, what?

# CHAPTER 15

Riley struggled through the week. His mind was not on his work. He was more than happy when the week was over. He would spend the night in Amarillo with Joyce, and they would leave early the next morning for Lake City.

"Well, how did your two weeks go?"

"Pretty good, I guess. The boss wasn't too happy that I was leaving. It seems they have a difficult time keeping proofreaders. A few more dollars on the paycheck might help."

"That's one thing you won't have to worry about at the *Weekly Standard*."

"What's that?"

"A payroll check."

"I don't quite know how to take that. Is that good or bad?"

"Depends largely on your performance. Remember, you'll be getting room and board to go along with it."

"Remember Mr. Hughes, half of everything you have is now mine. Perhaps you should reconsider this salary issue."

"I can see I'm in for some tough negotiations."

"That you are."

"Lemme see, now. If half of what I have is yours, then you have fifty percent of what I have. Right?"

"Right, Mr. Hughes. Right."

"Now then, I also have fifty percent of what you have. Right?"

"Right."

"Then if I have fifty percent of your fifty percent, that leaves you with twenty-five percent. Right?"

"And you passed the third grade? Hard to believe."

Riley grinned. "Well, I made an 'A' in recess. At any rate, I'm glad you're coming home. I have to admit, I missed you these past two weeks."

"And I missed you, Riley. Now we can look forward to the future, and I'm thinking this trip to Lake City will be great. I hate to admit it, but Amarillo is as far as I have been from Madden Grove."

"I haven't exactly been around the world myself."

It was a night for small talk and a time for making love. An early morning breakfast and they were on their way to Lake City. It was a beautiful drive from South Fork, Colorado to Lake City, the highway, such as it was, winding alongside the Rio Grande.

Several miles past the old mining town of Creede they left the Rio Grande Valley and began to climb into even higher elevations. The air was cool and brisk, a far cry from the flat land of southern Oklahoma. They stopped several times along the way to take pictures and admire the scenery. They enjoyed a picnic lunch within view of waterfalls on Clear Creek as the water came thundering over a cliff to the valley below.

"Gee, I think I could live up here."

"Not in the winter time. According to the article in the paper, they get several feet of snow a year. I'd get claustrophobia stuck in a cabin all winter."

"I suppose you're right, but I have never seen any prettier country than this."

The trip into Lake City over the continental divide and the view of the sparkling waters of Lake San Cristobal from high in the mountains was beauty Riley and Joyce had only seen in pictures. Riley was glad he brought a camera.

T-Mountain Lodge was nestled among aspen trees half way up a small mountain overlooking the Lake Fork of the Gunnison River. Cabins were sparsely furnished, a bed, shower, table, chairs, a cook stove and a few utensils.

"Rustic."

"Yeah, it sure is, but I guess it serves the purpose. I really didn't expect a Holiday Inn. Let's take in the town before it gets dark. We'll see if we can find a café for supper and buy some groceries for the next few days."

Taking in the town didn't take long. Lake City was the county seat of Hinsdale County, one of the least populated in the nation. Downtown consisted of a grocery store, service station, several souvenir shops, a café, and more than ample bars.

Joyce located the courthouse. "This is where they tried Alfred Packer for the murder of his comrades. There was no town here at the time, and they came over the mountains with pack mules in search of minerals and got caught in a winter storm. As the story goes, the men ran out of food and Packer killed them, one by one, and ate them. A pretty gory story, isn't it?"

"Yes it is. I'm not sure I could ever get that hungry."

Even so Riley managed to down his share at the dinner table. It had been a long day, and bedtime came early.

"Hard to believe, having to light a fire to stay warm in the middle of the summer."

"I'd hate to have to pay the propane bill up here in the winter. I wonder if they have anybody who comes up here or spends the winter."

"Deer hunters, I imagine. But I don't know anyone from Oklahoma who would want to come up here to hunt deer. We have plenty. I bet I've seen a hundred or so hanging around Red River."

Joyce snuggled close to Riley. "You're warm as toast." She put her cold feet against his legs.

"Gads, woman. Your feet are cold."

"That's why I got them against you—so I can get them warm."

Riley pulled Joyce closer. "I love you very much Miss Joyce. But I'm thinkin' I'm gonna buy you some muffins for your cold feet."

Joyce giggled and snuggled even closer. The two fell asleep in each other's arms.

Riley awoke to the smell of fresh brewed coffee mingled with cool mountain air.

"Get up lazy bones. I'll fix breakfast, but that's it. Remember, I'm on vacation, too."

Riley sat on the edge of the bed, rubbing his eyes. "Gee, that coffee smells good." He peeked out the window toward the river. "It's beautiful. If I was a painter, I would have a field day up here."

"What do you propose we do today?"

"I've got a couple folding chairs in the trunk of the car. Let's pack a picnic lunch and go up by the lake. Just sightsee, maybe."

"I'd like to make some of the souvenir shops downtown."

"Typical female. We'll do it."

An hour and a half of wandering in and out of stores, picking up half the items and examining them, confirmed what Riley's father had taught him long ago: turn a woman loose in a store and she can spend hours just looking, whether she buys anything or not. And the old gent was right. Joyce bought nothing.

The road paralleled the river as they drove to the lake. Riley stopped twice along the route to watch the clear mountain water rush down the river.

"I wish we had something like this back home. I'm afraid old Beaver Creek will never be this clear."

"That's for sure."

Riley pulled the folding chairs from the trunk of his car, and he and Joyce sat beside the lake. They could see snow on the high mountains and across the lake smoke rose from the chimney of a cabin. A single fisherman was trolling down the lake. Riley sat in silence.

"You seem preoccupied."

"I what?"

"I said you seem to be somewhere else. Something on your mind?"

"Maybe so. Do you know Farley Branson?"

"Never heard of him. What does he do?"

"I'm not sure. He says he is an officer in a bank down in south Texas."

"How do you know him?"

"He preached one Sunday for Rev. Crampton. When I tried to take his picture for the newspaper, he said he didn't want his picture taken. I can't see what difference it makes. Most people would welcome a little good publicity, but not this guy. I am sure I saw him once in Duncan, and he was at the Terral Watermelon Festival."

"So?"

"Somehow that just doesn't ring true. He said his father is a preacher who heard Rev. Crampton was retiring and he stopped by to see him on his way to Kansas City. He showed up in Duncan. I'm almost sure that it was Farley, unless he has a twin brother. He was talking to some guy, and when I came back around the corner, he was gone. Then he shows up at Terral. It just doesn't add up."

"What do you think he does?"

"That I don't know."

"Did you ever think about checking with the bank to see if he works there?"

"I thought about it, but on second thought, I don't guess it is any of my business."

"Well, maybe it is exactly as he said. He works for a bank, and he just doesn't want his picture taken."

"Oh well, I guess it's not that important, one way or the other."

The picnic lunch didn't last long, and Riley suggested they return to T Mountain before dark. "I don't want to run into a bear in the middle of the night."

When Riley and Joyce arrived back at the cabin they noticed a Texas license plate on a car in the next cabin. A pair of fishing waders was hanging on a line. A man in his early thirties was sitting in a chair, leaning back against the cabin wall.

As Riley stepped from his car, he spoke to the man. "You fellows catching any?"

"Oh yeah. We caught a big mess today."

"I notice you're from Texas. Whereabouts?"

"We're from Wichita Falls."

"We're from Ryan, just across the river."

"Well, it's a small world. My name is Don Pilcher. My partner is in the kitchen cooking trout." He turned and yelled at this partner. "Hey, George, come out here. We got some neighbors you'll want to meet."

Pilcher turned to Riley. "George is from Beaver Valley. Maybe you'll know him."

George emerged from the cabin, spatula in hand. "Did I hear my name called?"

"That you did. Meet these people from Ryan. You do know where Ryan is?"

"Naturally. I'm George O'Neal."

Riley introduced himself and Joyce. "This is our first trip up here. It's one beautiful place."

Don smiled. "Yes it is. George and I come up here every year to trout fish. We never fail to catch fish here. It's a race to see who can catch the most and the biggest. Naturally, he comes in second."

"Bull! If you believe that, you believe in Santa Claus."

George addressed Riley. "I guess I should know you. I graduated from Beaver Valley high ten years ago. Were you always from Ryan?"

"Yes, my father owned the *Weekly Standard*. He has retired, and we have it."

"I know the name. Don and I are police officers from Wichita Falls. I try to keep up with what's going on around Beaver Valley. I see where Buster Phillips is to be tried for the murder of the second grade teacher. I never knew him. He came about two years after I graduated. I used to go to some of the games he coached. It's a sad thing."

"Yes it is. No one would have ever thought of him doing such a thing. I understand they will be selecting a jury in a week or so. What's happening in Wichita Falls?"

"I guess you've heard about the serial killer, the one who strangles women with a rope. We had one happen in Wichita Falls the night before we left. They think it's the work of the serial killer. Seems he always uses a rope to strangle them, and there is alcohol involved. I'm sure there are other similar things in the deaths, but we don't know what they are just yet."

"With the trial of Buster coming up and the serial murders, that's not the type of news you like to hear."

"No, it isn't. Have you folks had dinner?"

"No. We were on our way to the cabin to see what we could scrounge up—or go into town to find something."

"Why don't you eat with us? We have more trout than Don can eat. I don't eat them. We give away a lot more than he eats. I've got the skillet hot, plenty of fried potatoes, salad and cream corn."

"Sounds great to us."

It was a satisfying meal. George was a good cook, and Don ate a pan full of rainbow trout by himself.

"I catch 'em. He eats 'em."

That brought a round of laughter and a rebuke from Don.

# CHAPTER 16

It was a very good week. A trip up Henson Creek to an abandoned mine, then up into the high meadows highlighted the week. A gravel road wound around the mountainside, often dipping within a few feet of the creek. The creek, though small, ran fast and furious, skipping over boulders, gathering at times in small pools, then rushing on toward the river.

Joyce had prepared a picnic lunch, and the two of them sat on a large flat boulder next to the stream. Riley dipped a cup into the cold mountain water.

"I don't think you would do this in Beaver Creek—drink out of it."

"Not hardly."

The gravel road wound further into the highlands and opened into a broad expanse. Several small cabins, most without roofs and windows, abandoned many years past, were stark reminders of what must have been hard times in the lives of miners of a bygone era.

"Golly, I wonder how anybody could survive up here in the winter living in something like that—a one room shack half buried in the ground. They must have been hardly souls."

"No doubt about it. The article in the *Globe* said places like this didn't last too long." Joyce shrugged. "According to the paper, no one stays up here in the wintertime. The only people here are Basques from Spain who live with the sheep during the summer. They herd them down from the mountains when the snows begin, I guess to be shipped to market."

A light mist began to fall in the higher elevations and Riley turned the car toward the valley. "I guess we better head in to the cabin before we get caught up in some bad weather. I remember Don said it gets bad in a hurry. He said they came up here late in

September one year and barely got out ahead of a snowstorm. Not much chance of that now, but it's time to head in."

A honeymoon and a vacation, both wrapped up in one. It was the best of times. Don brought a large mess of trout the next day.

"We catch more than I can eat. George doesn't eat them, and we don't want to carry them back to Texas."

Saturday came, and they left for home, spending the night in Amarillo and loading the remainder of Joyce's belongings in the two cars and driving back to Oklahoma Sunday. It was a great time, and the two vowed to make the trip again the following year.

"I wonder what's been happening back home."

Riley grinned. "What could possibly happen? The cakewalk and the Watermelon Festival are over. I don't know. Some people think it's not much fun living in a small community where nothing exciting ever happens, but I am thinking I much prefer it to the hustle and bustle of a big city. Traffic you can't imagine, murders, robberies, rapes and the Good Lord knows what else. No ma'am, I'll take our lifestyle anytime. The only thing I can think of coming down the pike is the upcoming school bond election and the trial of Buster Phillips."

"That's pretty sad, the trial of the coach."

"Yes it is. I barely know the man but, it's hard to see how in the world he could do such a thing. I think everyone else feels the same way. I know Coach Park is pretty upset about it. They are pretty close."

It was a long drive home. They unpacked and found something to eat. When it was all through, Riley gazed at the bed. It was a welcome site.

Monday mornings were Monday mornings, and Riley wondered what the next week would bring. Joyce would work with Sara, gathering the local news. It was the *Weekly Standard's* turn to publish the county commissioner's proceedings again.

"Before you go," said Sara, "we finally got a preacher, and he's a good one. He was well respected in his church and in the community. He lost his wife within the past year, and he felt it would better for him to find a new church, perhaps start over. I know it must be a real tragedy for him, but I think he will be fine. I know the elders and the congregation are well pleased. You will have to come and hear him."

"I'll take the camera and get a picture when I get back from Beaver Valley. We'll have it in the paper next week."

Riley drove to Beaver Valley and the courthouse for the proceedings and to see what might have transpired while he was away.

Sitting behind her desk in the judge's office, a petite young lady was typing speedily, peering over thick glasses.

"What's happening, Four Eyes? You're gonna burn that typewriter up if you don't slow down."

Faith Harris peered over her glasses at Riley. "You know how the judge is. He gives you something tomorrow and wants it yesterday. What are you doing in our town, snooping again?"

"Well, yes and no. I came to pick up the county commissioner's proceedings. What's happening exciting in the county seat?"

"I guess the big news is the selection of a jury for the Buster Phillips trial. They are in the process of doing that now. I would imagine the trial will start sometime next week."

As Riley turned to leave the office, Faith had more to say.

"Listen Riley, you need to keep your old girlfriend in your town."

"What are you talking about? And who might that be?"

"Maurine."

"Yes gads. What's she done now?"

"She was in a fight with Prissy Bradford up at the bar in Addington. It took two deputies, the bartender and a highway patrolman to break it up."

"I guess she was drunk again."

"Is there any time when she isn't?"

"I guess she's in the local jail."

"You got it. I suppose you will want to bond her out?"

"No ma'am. You got her. You can keep her. And by the way, she's not my girlfriend and never was. I graduated with her, and that's the extent of it."

Faith chuckled. "Get out of here, Riley. I've got work to do."

Riley went to the sheriff's office for the weekly report and check on the upcoming trial. Sheriff Aten was reading reports.

"What's happening on the crime scene, AA?"

"Right now Eddie and Howard are out on Highway 5 near Hastings. Old man Brenner's cows are out again. I've told him more than once to get his fences mended. Somebody is going to run into one of them one of these days, and the old man is going to be in trouble."

"Have they seated a jury for the Phillips case?"

"No, not yet. I don't know how many have been selected. It's a tough one. Everyone knows Buster, and some of the prospective jurors will be disqualified. Even so, I imagine it will be done by tomorrow."

"Did his attorney ask for a change of venue?"

"No. I think he felt Buster had a better chance here. This is a capital case, you know, and I think he feels people in the county would not return a death penalty. But then again, who knows?"

Riley's drive back to the *Weekly Standard* was filled with thoughts of Buster Phillips and the horrible crime for which he was accused. He had picked up on the motive, a one-sided love affair. Even so, killing someone you love was something hard to comprehend. He would be at the trial next week.

Roger was sitting at the Linotype with Missy in his lap.

"You're gonna spoil that rotten cat."

"She's hard to refuse."

"I've brought back the county commissioner's proceedings. State law requires they be published. There are a lot of figures. I think you can handle it now. You'll need to check a file copy to set how they are set. This is one item that allows for no errors. Take your time, and read each line before you send it in. Joyce will do the proof reading when you get through. I'll be back sometime after lunch. I'm going to meet the new preacher and get a picture for next week's issue."

"He's a good one."

"Then you were at last Sunday's sermon? From what Sara says, everyone seems to be well pleased with him."

"Mom was impressed. And I think Rev. Crampton is happy and looking forward to retirement."

Riley called the church and the new pastor answered.

"I'll be here."

# CHAPTER 17

"Terrance Williams, Mr. Hughes. Everyone calls me Terry."

The two men shook hands. Terrance Williams was a short, stocky man with a slightly receding hairline and horn-rimmed glasses.

"I'm more than happy to meet you, Terry, and I'm Riley. My dad is Mr. Hughes. You've only been here a little more than a week, and I have already heard some good words about you."

"I must have somebody fooled. Have a seat."

"I'd like to get a picture and do an article, Terry. We always try to put out the word when a new pastor or teacher arrives in town. We're a small newspaper, but in a town this size, it's what I call the voice of the community."

"I understand. My experience has been in small towns, and I've found the newspapers are very cooperative and do an excellent job."

"First, I'd like to ask what brings you to Ryan?"

Terry Williams had a sad, almost melancholy gaze, which vanished as quickly as it appeared.

"I was very happy in my last church, Riley. But sometimes things happen in a man's life that calls for change. It is difficult for me to discuss it, but I think you need to know. I lost my wife about a year ago. I loved her as much as any man ever loved a woman. We were as happy a couple as there ever was.

"At first I cried myself to sleep every night. I could think of nothing but her. I had complete support from both the church and the community, but when I would see a familiar face, it might remind me that that person's child was in my wife's Sunday school class. It was all I could do to keep from breaking down, no matter where I was.

"Have you ever been in love, Riley?"

"Yes. I guess I am. I have just recently married."

"Cherish the moment. One never knows when life will suddenly come to an end. My wife had gone shopping and was involved in an automobile accident. She died on the way to the hospital."

"I'm sorry to hear that."

"Yes. But it will be with me always. I just can't seem to accept the fact that she is gone. I am forty-two years old. We had been married seventeen years, and it was a time filled with love. She was a true angel on earth, and I know God has called her home. But my heart aches. Never a day or time passes that she is not on my mind. She was a beautiful lady, Riley, and words can't tell you how much I loved her. It has been said that time is a great healer, but so far—well, I know you didn't come to hear of my sorrow."

"I know it must have been devastating."

"Yes it was, and is. But that, in large part, is why I am here. There were so many things that reminded me of her, the home, the church, the congregation and the people in town. I felt I might be better off with a change of scenery. I heard Rev. Crampton was retiring and thought this might be the change I needed. I talked to Rev. Crampton. He is an outstanding, quality person. I interviewed, and the deacons offered me the position."

"I think you will like our little community. Not a lot goes on here. We have the annual Rattlesnake Hunt up at Beaver Valley, the Watermelon Festival at Terral and a cakewalk here in the summer." Riley grinned. "Now that's top entertainment you won't find in many other places."

"Sounds like a real laid back community."

"It is. Nothing much ever happens around here, and that makes for some easy living. We have a school bond election coming up in September. The state fire marshal has threatened to condemn the grade school building, so we are having a big push to get the vote out, in favor obviously."

"Sounds like a worthy project."

"Yes, it is. The only other thing going on now is the upcoming trial of Buster Phillips, the basketball coach at Beaver Valley. He is accused of the murder of Pat Foster, the second grade teacher. It took place around Christmas time this past year."

"Rev. Crampton was telling me about it. Hard to believe."

"What's on your agenda this coming week?"

"John Crampton said he will take me to the county hospital tomorrow. He goes there once a week if anyone from Ryan is there. Of course we have prayer meeting on Wednesday. I plan on setting aside Thursday evening to visit in the local rest home and, as John has, conduct a prayer meeting. I'll do a little home visitation for any member of the congregation who is shut in."

"Sounds like a busy schedule."

"You'd be surprised. A pastor has a lot more to do than the regular Sunday and Wednesday meetings. I enjoy the work. It gives me a chance to visit with people and perhaps do somebody some good. It can be very rewarding at times."

"What do you do outside your work? Do you hunt or fish or have a hobby?"

"I like to fish when the opportunity presents itself."

"Do you know Roy Evans?"

"No."

"He's the local deputy sheriff and a very good friend. Roy and I occasionally set trotlines in Red River. We have caught some pretty good catfish from time to time. Perhaps you would like to go with us some Friday afternoon. We usually stay late, so we always take Coleman lanterns. It offers a change of pace."

"I'd like that, Riley. I really would."

"Great. I'll tell Roy. Maybe he can make arrangements with the sheriff for that time off, and we'll see about catching old man catfish."

Riley took his pictures and started toward the door. He hesitated and turned around to face Terry. "By the way, do you know a Farley Branson?"

"Farley Branson? No, I don't guess I have ever heard of him. Who is he?"

"Just a fellow I ran across. Matter of fact, he appeared before the church congregation not so long ago. I thought you might know him."

"No, I guess not."

As Riley was returning to the newspaper office, he suddenly recalled that John Crampton had said he did not know Farley Branson's father. While Branson had not said so, the inference was that he did. Perhaps it was only through church circles and not personally. John Crampton would, under no circumstances, lie. However, he might know more about Farley Branson he let on. But what was the connection? And, if John Crampton knew more than he was telling, why the big secret? What was so important about a jackleg preacher who claimed he was a bank vice-president? And what is the connection between Branson and John Crampton? How was it that he simply 'showed up' to make a presentation before the church congregation?

If John Crampton did not know Branson's father, the initial contact must have been by Branson. But for what reason? Why was Branson in Duncan when Riley went to purchase the office chair? What was he doing at the Terral Watermelon Festival? Surely he wasn't there just to eat watermelon. He was seen visiting with John Crampton.

A seemingly endless string of questions raced through Riley's mind. He had previously discussed the matter with Rev. Crampton and did not want to put the good reverend on the defensive. Whatever the relationship, it must be important. Perhaps he would never know, but a newspaperman by nature is inquisitive and Riley was certainly no exception. "Perhaps," he thought, "I will just lay behind the log. Maybe someday, some time, the answer will come."

Some things never changed. When Riley arrived at the office, Sara was, as usual, talking on the telephone. Joyce was sitting at the other desk, taking it all in. It never ceased to amaze Riley how long a female newspaper reporter could talk to one person on the phone. Sara was the master.

Roger was busy setting the county commissioner's proceedings on the Linotype. Missy, her usual pesky self, was rubbing against his leg, hoping for some attention.

"Well, I met the new preacher. We'll have his picture and an article in next week's paper."

Roger looked up from the machine. "He sure seems like a nice person. He was really impressive last Sunday."

"He's got some big shoes to fill with John Crampton's retirement. By the way, he said he likes to fish. I think the next time I see Roy I'll see if he wants to take the new pastor to the river to do a little trotlining. Would you like to go with us?"

"Yes, sir. I'd like that."

"If nothing happens, perhaps we can go this Friday afternoon. I'll see if I can run Roy down."

Riley had no sooner said it than Roy walked in the back office.

"What's up, Roy?"

"They've seated a jury. Buster Phillips' trial starts tomorrow. I thought you would want to know."

"Yeah. I'll make as much of it as I can. Roger is coming along pretty well on the Linotype. We may have to work a little late, but this has got to be the biggest news story in the county in a long time."

Riley remembered the fishing trip. "By the way, the new preacher, Terry Williams, said he would like to go fishing with us sometime. What say we go this coming Friday afternoon, if I don't get hung up on the Phillips trial? Roger wants to go with us. I suspect a young scout like him can handle one end of the minnow seine as good or better than any of us."

"I'll check with AA and get back with you."

As Roy was leaving, Joyce came to the back office. "I heard that. You haven't been married a month and you are already abandoning your bride in favor of a fishing trip."

Riley grinned. "Sometimes a man has just gotta do what he's gotta do. Besides, we want to make a favorable impression on our new preacher."

Joyce laughed. "I guess I'll just have to play second fiddle to a catfish."

"Not for long, my dear, only this Friday evening. You do like catfish, don't you? Remember, half of what I have is yours and I'll be more than willing to share my part of the catch with you."

"You are a true romanticist. How could I reject such an offer?"

"I knew you would see the right side of it."

It would be a two-day trial for Buster Phillips. Riley sat in a packed courtroom. Buster did not take the stand in his defense. The evidence was overwhelming, and Buster's own admission prior to the trial seemed to dictate a foregone conclusion. Buster seldom looked up, staring at the table in front of him. His wife sat in the back of the courtroom with tears in her eyes. It was a heart-wrenching ordeal for her, and Riley wondered what would become of her and the children. He knew she would not remain in Beaver Valley, and Roy seemed to think she would return to Arkansas where her parents lived.

The jury returned a guilty verdict and retired to the jury room to determine the punishment. There was only two options, death or life imprisonment. The jury opted for life imprisonment and those in the courtroom breathed a sigh of relief. Buster Phillips was well liked and respected in the community. He made a terrible mistake and now he had to pay the price.

Formal sentencing was the job of a reluctant Judge Harris.

"James A. 'Buster' Phillips, it is the recommendation of a jury of your peers that you be sentenced to life in prison for the murder of Pat Foster. It is with regret that I pronounce that sentence. You have been a leader in your community and have enjoyed the trust and respect of the youth of this wonderful community. You have betrayed that trust. It is a betrayal that will be with you from this day forward. You are hereby remanded to the custody of the sheriff of this county until such time as you will be transferred to the custody of the Oklahoma Department of Corrections.

"This court is adjourned."

It would be "old news" by the time the article appeared in the following week's newspaper. Several large dailies were represented in the courtroom, and the wire service would send the news across the wires to every major news outlet in the nation. Even so, it would be front page for the *Weekly Standard* and a major topic of discussion in the county for some time to come.

But now, a fishing trip to Red River with the new pastor.

# CHAPTER 18

"Have you ever been trotlining before, Terry?"

"Not in a river. I've done a little bottle fishing in some of the Texas lakes, and I'm afraid my trotlining experience is limited. Most of the time I sat on the bank of a stock tank."

"The first thing we have to do is catch some bait. We'll seine minnows out of the shallows and set the lines just above the drifts. Catfish stay in the deeper water and seem to come out to feed in the shallows late in the evening.'

"Ever catch any big ones?"

"There are some in the river but we seldom catch those. I think the largest we have caught on the trotlines was something like ten pounds. Even so, that's quite a fish."

Roger and Riley seined for minnows as Roy and Terry set the lines above several drifts. The river minnows were easy to catch, and the lines were soon baited. The men retired to a sandbar, and the conversation turned to the trial and conviction of Buster Phillips.

"It had to be one of the shortest murder trials on record, only two days."

"Well," said Roy, "the evidence was pretty strong against him. He didn't take the stand, and I guess he was resigned to his fate."

"I guess so. What do you think Terry? From what I could gather, Buster was a well-respected man in the community. He taught a Sunday school class and was very active in the community. I didn't know him well, but I've never heard a word spoken against the man."

"From what little I've heard, it was a love affair. John Crampton told me the report he got was that Buster fell in love with her, but she rejected him. I can't imagine murdering someone you love. It is beyond my comprehension."

"I think that's true for most of us." Riley shook his head. "I don't guess anyone will ever know what goes on in the mind of someone else."

Terry turned and stared down the river. "This is true. Sometimes I guess a man just snaps. I am sure he was a good man who lost control of his emotions. Sometimes something will set us off, and we will do something we would not do under normal conditions. I guess when she rejected him, if that is the case; it was more than he could bear. He might not have even known what he was doing."

The men ate sandwiches and built a fire from driftwood washed in during flood stages. Fishing was better than average, and by ten o'clock two stringers were loaded with catfish.

"Quite a catch," said Terry. "I never thought we'd have this kind of luck."

"Sometimes it happens, sometimes it doesn't. Maybe you've brought us good luck."

"I guess by the time we get home and clean fish it will be midnight. I don't know about the two of you, but I think Roger and I will sleep in. We don't have a lot to do this Saturday, other than melting the lead, and I think I have one envelope job to do."

Terry laughed. "I remember the song 'Give me five minutes more of your time, don't you know that Sunday morning you can sleep late?' Well, Saturday morning is my sleep late morning. I appreciate you fellows letting me tag along. It was a most enjoyable evening."

"We're glad to have you. You handle a mean dip net. Perhaps we can go again sometime soon." Roy smiled. "We don't have a lot of the entertainment you find in the big cities. We sort of have to make our own and fishing and hunting makes for the most of it."

"Thanks, Roy. Now I'll invite you and Riley to come to the service Sunday. I know Roger will be there, as will his mother."

Riley arrived home with several catfish as Joyce was preparing for bed.

"Here you are, fresh from Red River."

"What do you mean 'here you are'?"

"I thought you might want to clean these so we can have them for dinner tomorrow."

Riley knew it was coming. "Mr. Hughes, if you want catfish for dinner tomorrow you better head for the back porch and clean them."

"Here now. I have labored long and hard to provide you with dinner. You are a taskmaster."

Joyce stuck a bony finger in Riley's ribs. "To the back porch, Mr. Hughes."

Riley grinned. "Come. I'll show you how to do this. There is definitely an art to it."

Joyce followed Riley to the porch with no intention of cleaning fish.

"What do you think about the new preacher?"

"He seems like a nice man. I think he will fit in this community just fine. The church is fortunate to have him, and I know Rev. Crampton will be happy now that he can turn the reins over to someone else."

"What's on the agenda for tomorrow?"

"I told Roger to sleep in. We'll get to the office about ten. He can do the melting, and I have an envelope job to do. It should be a short day, unless something comes up."

"You smell like a catfish. I hope you plan on taking a bath before you get in bed with me. If not, you can sleep on the couch."

"Yes, ma'am."

"Yes, ma'am? Does that mean you are going to take a bath or sleep on the couch?"

Riley held up his hands and moved toward Joyce as she backed into the kitchen.

"You better not touch me. You might sleep on the couch, bath or no bath."

Riley chuckled as he went to the shower.

It was good to sleep in. Saturdays in the newspaper office, for the most part, were slow. When Riley arrived at the office, Roger had a broom in hand and a fire was under the melting pot.

"You're early. I thought you would want to sleep in."

"I had to clean the fish last night and didn't get in bed until nearly midnight, but Mom always wakes up early. If I wanted any breakfast, I had to get up with her."

"What do you think about the new preacher?"

"I like him. He really is a good speaker. Mom likes him, too. Matter of fact, she has invited him over for a catfish dinner."

"Ruth Hayes," thought Riley. "Hmmm. Maybe this could be the beginning of a budding romance. Who knows? Ruth, in her late thirties, had been single for some fifteen years and was a very nice looking person with a good personality. And the reverend had recently lost his wife. It could be a good match."

Riley knew Terry was lonely and missed his wife. Ruth had been alone for a number of years, and Riley often wondered why she hadn't found someone. Maybe, just maybe, something would come of it.

Roger finished sweeping and began the weekly ritual of pouring the lead into molds for the Linotype. Riley printed a box of envelopes.

"Let's call it a day, Roger. We're in pretty good shape for next week. We'll have Terry's picture and story on the front page, along with Buster's trial. Quite a contrast. You can set the governor's report on Monday. By the way, when does school start?"

"The middle of next month."

"You can come in after school and on Saturday. By next summer you will be able to run this place by yourself."

Joyce had invited Riley's parents for dinner. The elder Hughes was quick to add that catfish and hushpuppies were his favorite. Riley's mother had baked a cherry pie. It was indeed a good time.

The word was out that a new preacher was in town, and Sunday morning the church was packed. The women were dressed in their finest, and the men wore suits to greet the new preacher. Arlene Manning played the piano, and the rich tenor voice of James Bolden rang out with a beautiful hymn. Rev. Crampton offered a short prayer and, as he had the previous week, welcomed Terry Williams as the new pastor.

In his times in the church, limited though they were, Riley had never heard a better sermon. He whispered to Joyce. "He is really good."

"Yes, he is, the best I have heard. I'm surprised he is not in some big church somewhere."

As the congregation filed out the door, Terry was on hand to greet them, along with Rev. Crampton.

Riley shook Terry's hand. "A great sermon, Terry."

"Well, thank you, Riley. I might do a little better in the pulpit than I do running trotlines, but I've had a lot more experience with the former."

Rev. Crampton beamed. "I knew you would be pleased. I don't think the deacons could have selected a better man for the job. This church will always be in my heart, and I feel great, knowing that it will be in good hands."

It was a warm, lazy Sunday afternoon, a time to relax before the start of the new week. Joyce was at the kitchen table, thumbing through her grandparent's family album. Riley sat in his easy chair, reading a western novel and was soon fast asleep.

When Riley and Joyce arrived late Monday morning, Sara was already on the phone. Roger was at the Linotype.

"What did you think about the new preacher?"

"I thought he was really good. How did the catfish dinner go?"

Roger grinned. "Rev. Williams can eat his weight in catfish. He and Mom really seemed to hit it off. I like him. He's funny. I left to go to town, and he and Mom sat on the porch swing and visited. They were still talking when I got home."

"Yeah. He does seem like a nice guy. We'll have to take him with us again when we go to the river. I think he enjoyed it. I know that he enjoys his work, but sometimes it is good to get away from it now and then. I also noticed that Rev. Crampton seems well pleased with him."

Maybe it is a budding romance, Riley thought. Terry had lost his wife a year ago, and Ruth had been alone for some time. It could be the end of a lonesome time for two people. Time would tell.

# CHAPTER 19

Tom Smart was in his office when Riley made his weekly trip to the funeral home.

"I heard Lottie Hamilton passed away this week."

"Yes. She was ninety-three. It didn't come as a surprise. Bob over at the rest home told me last week she was in pretty bad shape. But Lottie isn't the only one. Sidney Roberts died this morning. He was seventy-six."

"Sounds like you're gonna be busy."

"Well, we expected these two could go any time, but I don't guess you heard about Freddie Wilson."

"No. What happened to him?"

"Apparently he had been over to Wichita Falls, and was on his way home. According to the information I got, he was drunk and tried to beat the Rock Island engine across Highway 70 at Beaver Valley and didn't make it. The train dragged his pickup all the way to the depot before they could get it shut down. It made a mess out of Freddie, one of the worst I've seen."

"That's sad. I don't think I could handle your business, Tom."

"It can be a little disheartening at times. Death comes to us all sooner or later. I don't know that there is a good part to it, but we do our best to console the families. In the case of Lottie, it isn't so bad. She lived a full life, but it gets tough in cases like Freddie. He was only thirty-seven."

"When a man gets full of liquor, he shouldn't get behind the wheel."

"That's true, but it's too late for Freddie."

"I guess the new preacher will have to conduct his first funeral service."

"I don't know about that yet. Rev. Crampton will conduct Lottie's service. She was a long time member of his church.

Freddie will be buried down at Terral, and they'll have a preacher down there conduct the service. I don't know about Sidney. His brother from Little Rock is due in tomorrow. He's the closet of kin, so he'll make that decision."

Riley walked back to the newspaper office. He wouldn't want Tom's job, and he couldn't see being a preacher, having to deal with all the problems of people and then conducting their final service. Maybe the newspaper profession wasn't so bad after all.

The week would be busy news-wise. Terry Williams' picture and story would be on the front page, along with the trial and conviction of Buster Phillips. Three obituaries and the big push for the school bond election would also be included.

Joyce was in the process of writing her first wedding anniversary under the watchful eye of Sara.

"Fifty years—that's a long time to be married to the same person."

Riley smiled. "Hang in there. We've already made the better part of a month of marriage."

"I'm working on it, Mr. Hughes."

Riley completed the obituaries and put them on the copy hook for Roger. "I guess I'll make the rounds, pick up the grocery ads and see what else I can drum up."

The first stop was always the "bench" leaning against Armstrong's Grocery on Highway 81, the main highway through town. Every town had its share of old timers, and for Ryan, the "bench" was their gathering place. Turn-of-the-century stories were always in abundance. Between whittling on a piece of wood, watching the traffic and a jaw full of chewing tobacco, the old timers could spin yarns that were, at times, hard to believe.

Riley always took the time to listen. He couldn't imagine life without automobiles and highways, but the old timers could recall such days, and Ed Walker particularly liked to tell of his first encounter with one of the "monster engines."

"The dad-burned thing scared my horse, and the next thing I knew I was layin' in a ditch. Things was a little slower then, and folks did a lot more visitin.' These here days folks just don't seem to have time, always on the go and never gettin' anything done. It just ain't the way it otta be."

"Yeah, I reckon that's so," piped in Brad Henderson. "I remember when Pa would hitch Macy to the wagon and we would come to town on trade's day. Seems like half the county was in town."

The old timers had a penchant for arguing just for the sake of arguing. Riley recalled one such argument between Ed James and Thomas Hopson. Both seemed to be masters at butchering the English language.

"You ain't never caught no fifty-three-pound catfish in Beaver Creek."

"The hell I ain't," replied Tomas. "Back in '42. Whatta mean I ain't caught no fifty-three pounder? You was there."

"No, I shore wasn't."

"Damn shore was."

"Wasn't."

Riley wondered if anyone back east would ever understand the local dialect. An English teacher was sure to shudder with just two minutes of conversation from "the bench."

Mondays would usually dictate the financial picture for the *Weekly Standard.* Riley would make his rounds of the business establishments, picking up the grocery ads, usually an ad from the dry goods store, a small ad from the theatre and a few more. This Monday would provide an additional push, as both the hardware store and the lumberyard were having sales.

"It's a good week for advertising." Riley sat at his desk. "It's better than usual." He grinned. "Maybe we can afford cheese on our hamburgers this week."

"We'll be pressed to get it all into eight pages this week," said Sara. "Margaret at the law firm in Beaver Valley called, and someone needs to pick up some legal advertising."

"I can do that," Joyce said. She added, "I've got to go by the real estate office and check on my house in Madden Grove. I'd sure like to sell it. Maybe Dame Fortune will smile on me."

"While you are there, pick up the sheriff's report and see if there is any other news around the courthouse."

It would be a tight squeeze to hold the week's issue to eight pages. Once a year the *Weekly Standard* printed a twelve-page graduation issue for the high school and a sixteen-page Christmas issue. Roger was improving daily, and Riley wondered why he had not hired a printer's devil in the past. It made his work a lot easier and gave him more time to hustle news and advertising.

Joyce returned from Beaver Valley in the middle of the afternoon. "I picked up the legal ad and the sheriff's report. The talk around the courthouse is still the trial of Buster Phillips. Sheriff Aten said they are awaiting the order to transfer him to the penitentiary at McAlester. Howard Roberts, the deputy, is sick about it. Buster was his high school coach."

"It will take a while but, like everything else, Buster's trial will fade into history and things will get back to normal. Matter of fact, it's normal for me to get a haircut once a month or so, and I think it is about due."

"Yeah. You are getting a little shaggy."

Early Tuesday morning Riley was in McMillion's Barber Shop. Coach Butler was in the chair.

"What are you getting all 'gussied up' for, Coach? Wife on your case to get a haircut?"

"That's part of it." Coach Butler, long time high school basketball coach, retired several years past, but he never missed a high school game and still managed to coach grade school softball. "I've been asked to be a pall bearer at Sidney Roberts' funeral. I'm gonna miss old Sidney. He and I had been friends for over forty years."

"Yeah. Lots of news around here this week." The old barber had been around even longer than the coach had. "Sidney and Lottie both gone. Seems like we're really losing a lot of the old timers here of late. And then there's Buster's trial, and I guess you heard about the woman being strangled over at Wichita Falls? They seem to think it's the same guy that killed the other women, the one at Bowie and down in Dallas and at Oklahoma City. A lot of news, but it ain't the kind of news you like to hear."

"Joyce and I heard about the murder over at Wichita Falls while we were in Colorado. A couple of Wichita Falls police officers were up there trout fishing, and they said it happened the night before they left. They didn't have any of the details."

Mac shook his head. "Makes you wonder if they're ever gonna solve those murders. Whoever is doing it is some kind of a nut. I hear none of them have been sexually assaulted. None of them have been robbed either. I heard the police found their purses in their cars and none of the money was taken."

"What do you think, Coach?"

"This guy must have some kind of a vendetta. From what I hear, there is always alcohol involved. I know it's not funny but some guys will get a woman drunk with the intent of having sex with her. But not this guy. Whatever a man does, he has a motive. I really wonder what motivates this guy."

Riley frowned. "I don't know. Maybe he's a sadist, and this is his sexual outlet. Who knows?"

Mac stirred the lather in the cup and dabbed soap around Butler's ears and neck. "Man, that guy has to be some kind of pervert, sexual or otherwise. I just can't imagine strangling people for no apparent reason."

"We may never know. It sure puts everyone on edge. No telling where he will strike next."

Mac finished cutting Coach Butler's hair. "That'll be fifty cents, Bob."

"Good grief Mac. That's double the price I paid the last time you cut my hair."

"So it is. But it has been a while since you had your hair cut. Besides, there is such a thing as inflation."

Riley grinned. "Pay up you old tightwad. Store-bought haircuts have been at fifty cents for six months. Where have you been?"

"My wife cuts my hair. Sometimes she falls a little short of Mac here. I thought since I had to be a pall bearer I didn't want to look like a shaved prune."

A smiling barber held out his hand as Coach Butler dug in his pocket for fifty cents.

"Come back, Coach."

Riley stepped into the chair.

"Short, like always, Mac."

"You know Riley, I think Coach is right. This serial killer must have some kind of a vendetta. I don't think I've ever heard of women being murdered, never sexually assaulted and nothing stolen from them. The motive sure isn't robbery. Weird."

"Yeah it is. Let's hope the police catch this rascal before he kills someone else."

# CHAPTER 20

It was a very good week. Wednesday night Roger was feeding the press with the first four pages, and Riley was at the make-up stone readying the second four. Missy was, as usual, rubbing against Riley's leg. He picked her up and placed her on the work stone.

"You are one pesky cat, always underfoot."

Roger finished the press run. "Man, I'm hungry. Mom's at prayer meeting tonight, so I guess I'll have to foot for myself when I get home."

"She kinda likes the new preacher, doesn't she?"

"Yes, she does. He's really a great speaker and seems like a real nice guy. I know one thing. He sure likes catfish."

"Maybe we can take him with us again soon. I'm hungry myself. I hope Joyce has fixed something good to eat."

Roger lifted the heavy lead forms from the press. It was a job for a young person, and Roger handled the forms with ease. Riley wondered once again why he had not hired a printer's devil in the past.

"Let's call it a day. I'll feed Missy. Let's go to the house."

Joyce was reading when Riley arrived home. "Where's my supper, woman?"

"Listen, Mr. Hughes. I worked hard three days this week, and I am relaxing. Besides, I haven't seen any paycheck with your signature on it. When do I get paid?"

"Paid? Paid? Woman you get paid every day with my undying love. How could you ask for anything more?"

Joyce laughed. "And I love you, too. But I can't go to the grocery store on that. You'll have to make do tonight with a sandwich. I'll go grocery shopping tomorrow."

"I guess Roger and I are in the same boat. He said his mother was at prayer meeting tonight, and he would have to fix his own. I'm thinking Ruth really likes Terry. At least Roger says she does."

"I think that's good. I know the preacher is lonely since he lost his wife. And I'm sure Ruth might well feel the same. Sometimes fate has a strange way of bringing people together."

"You are right. We sometimes think of preachers in different terms."

"How's that?"

"We seem to turn to them in times of trouble, times of grief, times when we need a shoulder to cry on. We forget they are people, just like us. They have feelings and they have troubles of their own. I know when I first met Terry I could tell he was devastated over the loss of his wife. I love you very much Joyce, and I know I would feel the same."

"I would feel the same if I lost you. It seems tragedies strike us all at one time or another. But I would rather look on the brighter side. We should do the things we enjoy and live life to its fullest."

"I agree with that for sure. Maybe this will work out for both Terry and Ruth. I know they both have had to face some pretty difficult obstacles. Let's hope for the best for both of them."

Riley ate his sandwich, took his shower and pulled back the covers. Wednesday was the longest workday of the week, and Riley felt it.

He awoke the next morning to the smell of coffee and sausage in the frying pan. "Golly, that smells good. I think I could eat a horse this morning."

"I'm fresh out of horse, but I'm going shopping this morning. What cut do you want, horseburger meat or horse hip roast? Whichever it is, I will need money, you know, m-o-n-e-y. Break loose, Scrooge."

Riley grinned. "I see your gonna be hard to deal with this morning." He pulled Joyce into his arms and kissed her. "I love you."

"I love you, too. Now fork over."

"Here's the checkbook. Armstrong is having a pretty good sale this week. I like to pass it around—maybe shop at Sanders next week. That's one thing Dad always taught me, don't shop at one store. They are all advertisers, and you need to pass it around."

"I can see that. What's on the agenda for the rest of the week?"

"I've got quite a bit of printing for the job press this week, letterheads, envelopes and some business cards. Roger and I will be busy tomorrow. I thought about asking Terry if he wanted to make another trip to Red River, but I talked to Roy and he said he couldn't make it this week. One of the deputies at Beaver Valley is on vacation and another had an aunt die out in the Texas panhandle. Maybe next week."

"Why don't we go over to Wichita Falls or to Duncan and take in a movie some Saturday?"

"Sounds good to me. The next time we have a reason to go to Wichita Falls we'll do it."

The *Weekly Standard* was in the post office Thursday by two o'clock. It was time for a cup of coffee, and Mabel placed the cup before Riley.

"Well now, how's the old married man? We don't see as much of you as we used to. Joyce won't let you out of the house?"

Riley laughed. "I could say she's a pretty mean woman, but she is a lot better cook than I am, so I've been eating at home. I like it that way."

Riley lifted the cup to his lips as Terry Williams sat down beside him.

"I see you are out and about, Reverend."

"Oh yes. I like a good cup of coffee now and then. I'm afraid I don't do too well in the kitchen."

"I talked to Roy and I was trying to get up another fishing trip to the river, but he has to work this Friday. Seems one of the deputies is on vacation and another had a relative die out of state. Maybe we can make it a week from Friday. Can you make it?"

"Sure, I'd love to go. I'm going to a little town north of Oklahoma City and spend the night with my sister. She and her husband have a new baby girl, and old uncle here wants to see her. I'll be back tomorrow afternoon."

"Your folks from Oklahoma?"

"No. My father has a farm near Waco. He and Mom have lived there all their lives. He inherited the farm from my grandfather."

"How did you decide to become a preacher?"

"I was in the Navy for four years. We had a chaplain that had an influence on my life. I have to tell you, Riley, that my life before I met that chaplain was not something that made my parents particularly happy. It's not that I was a criminal, but Dad is a Christian man, attends church every Sunday and I guess I was something of a backslider, a little wild at times."

"I guess we all go through that stage when we are young."

"I guess we do to some extent. The chaplain turned my life completely around. He is a wonderful man, a true believer, and he practiced what he preached. He asked what I planned on doing, maybe making a career out of the Navy. I told him I hadn't made up my mind what I was going to do. He asked me if I had ever considered the ministry." Terry Laughed. "He said I'd never find a better boss."

"Hard to argue with that."

"I thought about it. At first I wasn't really very interested, but as I watched the chaplain work, it occurred to me that he did a lot of good for a lot of young sailors. He was sort of like a father figure, always there when one of them had a problem, and he seemed to have an answer for their problems."

"I can see where a young fellow, really no more than a kid, away from home for the first time, could use a little advice and counsel from time to time."

"He sold me on it. When my enlistment was up, I decided to give it a try." Terry looked into his coffee cup as though he was a thousand miles away. "I enrolled in college, and that's where I met my wife."

Terry turned his head and looked away from Riley. He pulled a handkerchief from his pocket and wiped a tear from his cheek. "I'm sorry, Riley. I loved my wife so very much. It just doesn't seem fair that she is gone. Sometimes life deals us a tough hand, and it is hard to overcome it. I'm working on it, but it is something I have a problem with from time to time."

"I can sure understand that."

"We were in a history class together. She dropped her pen, and I bent over to pick it up for her. She bent over at the same time and we bumped heads." Terry tried to smile. "Hard to believe that two people met in such a manner. She smiled and told me I was hard headed. I guess she was right. We met in the history class for the rest of the semester, and toward the end of the semester I managed enough courage to ask her to have lunch with me. She accepted, and it just developed from there.

"I don't guess a man really knows how he falls in love or who he will fall in love with, but we really seemed to hit it off, even from the start. I don't guess there was ever a harsh word between us. I miss her, Riley, I really miss her."

"I know that no one can ever take her memory from you Terry, but you still have the rest of your life to live, and I'm sure your wife would want you to make the best of it."

"I'm trying Riley, I'm trying. I have asked Ruth to have dinner with me Saturday evening when I get back from my sister's place. I thought we might go up to Beaver Valley. She said the Casino Café has an excellent menu, so I thought we would try that."

"Ruth is a good person. She is a few years older than I am, and I know she has had it pretty tough, raising a boy by herself, maybe with a little help from her brother. I might say she has done an excellent job. Roger is a good boy and a hard worker. Maurice up at the school said he is an outstanding student. He's coming along quite well at the paper. He said he plans on going to college when he finishes high school. He will be able to find a job in most any university town. There is always a demand for Linotype operators."

"And what about you, Riley? I've told you my story, more or less. What are your plans?"

"As the old-timers would say, 'just keep on keepin' on.' My dad bought the newspaper back in the teens. Oklahoma had not been a state for very long, and he thought it might be a good place to live. He had been a printer back in Missouri. Everything was handset before the days of the Linotype. Mr. Daniel owned the *Weekly Standard*. He was getting along in years and needed some help, so he hired dad. Two years later his health began to fail, and he decided to sell the paper. Dad scraped up enough money to pay for part of it, and Mr. Daniel carried the rest.

"Mother's family always lived here, and they met and married. She worked at the paper three days a week, just like Sara and now Joyce. Even after I was born she had a little bed in the office for me. So I guess I have always been with the paper. It's all I know. I guess I'll be here until they cart me off."

Mabel poured a second cup of coffee. "Even if I tried to do something else I guess the printer's ink would always be with me."

The two men finished their coffee.

"I guess I better get on the road. It'll take me about three hours to get to my sister's place. Her husband will be home by then. He works in the oil field and puts in a lot of hours."

"I'll check with Roy and see if he can get some time off next week, and we'll catch old man catfish. I know Roger is rarin' to go."

"I'll be ready. See you Sunday in church?"

"We'll be there."

# CHAPTER 21

Sunday morning Riley and Joyce were dressing for church.

"I wonder how the dinner went with Terry and Ruth."

"What dinner?"

"Last Thursday after I put the paper in the post office I had coffee with Terry. He said he was on his way to see his sister near Oklahoma City. She had just had a baby and Terry wanted to see it. He also said that he had asked Ruth to have dinner with him at the Casino Café in Beaver Valley Saturday evening."

"I would imagine it went just fine."

"I'm sure it did, but Terry is having a difficult time over the loss of his wife. I know she has been gone for over a year now, but every time he thinks of her, you can tell there is a deep hurting inside the man. I don't know if he will ever get over it. Maybe his association with Ruth will help."

"Time takes care of a lot of things, Riley. He will never forget her, and he shouldn't. He'll just have to accept that she is gone and is not coming back. I think in time and with Ruth, he'll be fine."

"Let's hope so."

Reverend Williams was a dynamic speaker and was on his soapbox at the Sunday service. He preached long and hard against the evils of alcohol. He knew of the tragic death of Freddie Wilson, and while he did not mention Freddie's name, it was obvious he was referring to the train wreck that took his life.

The preacher was right. Little was to be gained with alcohol, particularly when it involved those who couldn't control it. It would be hard to argue against his message. Riley thought of the recent murders by the serial killer. Every one of the murders involved alcohol. He thought of his old classmate, Maurine, and her drunken bar fights. The local bar was always good for a drunk or two on Saturday night. Every town seemed to have a few who thought anytime was the right time to drink. Roy had mentioned that well over half the arrests made in the county related to alcohol, from public intoxication to driving under the influence. Charlie Two Horses and Black Jake spent more time in jail than most people did working during the week.

August was just around the corner. The average temperature in the last week of July was the hottest week of the year, and this year was no exception. With temperatures hovering between 105 and 110, it was difficult to find a cool place. Riley opened the double doors at the back of the newspaper office and placed a large fan facing the Linotypes. Monday was exceptionally hot. The heat from the lead pots made it uncomfortable, even with the fan at top speed.

"When you go to work on one of the dailies in a college town, they'll have a better cooling system than a floor fan."

Roger shook his head. "It is hot, isn't it? But I'll make out all right. Things ought to begin to cool off toward the end of next month. And school starts in another couple weeks."

"Are you on the basketball team this year?"

"No. I'd like to play, but I need to work, not only for the money, but to learn as much as I can. I want to go to college when I finish high school, and there won't be any money unless I am able to earn my own."

"I think that's a smart move. You'll have every afternoon after school to sweep and still have some time on the Linotype. On Saturday you can work on the machine after you do the melting. By the end of your senior year, you'll have it down pat."

"I hope so."

"Speaking of school, I have to attend the school board meeting tonight. They are planning on a final push for the grade school bond election. I am going to devote most of the front page to it. I have some information on the New London, Texas, school explosion some years back. If that doesn't convince the voters we need a new school building I don't know what will. If they don't approve it, we'll be holding school in the churches and the senior citizens center. That's all that's left. The fire marshal is sure to close the old building."

Roger grinned as he picked Missy up and scratched behind her ears. "I'll bet school board meetings are a lot of fun, especially with old man Kennedy in attendance. Man, he can talk the horns off a billy goat."

"I'd rather be fishing. Speaking of which, we're sort of planning on another trotlining trip to Red River this coming Friday evening. I think Roy will be able to make it, and I spoke to the preacher last week, and he said he's ready."

"I hope we have a good catch. I know Mom will be more than happy to cook them, and she'll invite Reverend Williams over for dinner. I get the good part. I get to clean 'em."

"They are seeing a lot of each other lately."

"Yes. She said the next time he comes for dinner she plans to invite Uncle Paul. I guess she wants her brother's approval to who she is seeing."

"I know Paul will be impressed. Well, I guess we can wrap things up around here. I'll feed Missy and see what I can talk the boss lady into fixing for dinner."

"It's sandwiches again tonight, Mr. Hughes. Two reasons: one, it's too hot to cook, and I've got to get ready for a baby shower tonight."

"Who is pregnant? Anyone I know?"

"It's Katie Simmons at Madden Grove. I think she is the only one up there young enough to have a baby."

"I thought she already had children."

"She does, four of them."

"That's nearly half the population of Madden Grove. If she has four kids, you'd think she would have enough baby clothes."

"All mothers want something new for their baby. Katie is no different. Besides, it's an opportunity to catch up on all the gossip."

"Women. I don't guess I will ever understand them."

"It doesn't look like it. Eat your sandwich."

"Come to think about it, I don't know whether I would rather go to a baby shower or to the school board meeting. Old man

Kennedy can bore you to tears. He never shuts up, and what he says doesn't amount to a hill of beans. He can be a pain in the butt."

Joyce grinned. "Enjoy yourself at the meeting."

"Yeah. Thanks."

School board meetings, like county commissioners meetings, like most all other meetings were boring. Riley thought boards meet just to see when they were going to meet again. But at least this meeting was important in that it would provide the final impetus for the bond election scheduled in early September.

Elvis Morris called the meeting to order.

The superintendent presented his usual report of happenings at the school since the last board meeting. "Not much new to report." Maurice chuckled. "Charlie Ward got his usual corporeal punishment last week."

"What's he done this time?"

"He brought a grass snake to school and turned it loose in the girls' restroom. Miss McKown heard screaming coming from the restroom and thought someone was hurt. I guess Charlie would have gotten away with it, but you know Charlie. He had to tell everyone. Miss McKown cleared the girls out of the restroom and Charlie was given the dubious duty of removing the snake, which had taken refuge behind one of the commodes."

Elvis and the board laughed. "How many spankings has Charlie had this semester?"

"Three that I can recall. He is always into something. I'm thinking he is an accident waiting to happen."

"Let's move on to the bond issue. I have a letter from the state fire marshal's office. If we don't move fast on this we'll be holding grade school in the parking lot. Riley, I assume we have your support on this. We will need all the favorable publicity we can get."

"You got it, Elvis. I plan on a large spread on the front page. I'm going to document the New London, Texas, grade school explosion, and I intend to draw a parallel to the condition of our grade school building. I can't imagine why anyone would vote against this bond issue."

"Don't bet on it, Riley. We've got a few folks in this town that are tighter than bark on a tree."

"I'm going to work with the merchants this week and see if they will sponsor an ad on the back page of the paper. I feel sure most of them will support the bond issue. Matter of fact, I don't know any of them who won't."

Dame Fortune smiled on the board, as Theodore Kennedy was absent, thus sparing members an hour of his constant babbling.

When Riley arrived home Joyce was pulling in the driveway.

"How did the big shower go?"

"It was a lot of fun. Katie got a lot of neat things for the baby. Sybil was there and she asked about you. I gave her lots of fodder."

"Thanks. I guess I'll be the talk of Madden Grove this week."

"I wouldn't be surprised."

"The school board meeting went off without a hitch. Old man Kennedy wasn't there. I plan on making the bond issue the big news story this week, that is, unless you and Sara preempt it in favor of Katie's baby shower."

"That is a thought. You gotta remember, Riley, half, maybe even more than half your readers are women. They want to hear about baby showers, who is visiting who, who is getting married, who is having a wedding anniversary and that sort of thing."

"They better be more concerned about the grade school bond election. If the old building blows up like the one in New London they'll have a lot more to worry about than a baby shower. I read the letter from the state fire marshal's office. He listed more problems with the old building than Carter has little liver pills."

"I don't think the board has anything to worry about. Women will vote in favor of the school bond." Joyce laughed. "If I remember right, women had a rather significant part in bringing these children into the world."

It was as Riley thought it would be. Not one merchant failed to support the bond issue with an ad. Both local banks purchased large ads. Even the rest home bought advertisement, and Riley was sure none of the residents would be attending school. Most community projects will be supported if justification is established. As promised, Riley devoted a large portion of the *Weekly Standard's* front page to the bond issue.

It was Sara's last week. Joyce would be on her own, gathering the society news, weddings, baby showers and the personal items.

"I don't know if I'll ever be as good as Sara. She knows everyone in town. You may wish you had her back."

"No. I think you'll do just fine. By the way, I hope you don't mind, but we're planning on a little fishing trip Friday evening. I talked to Roy and he said he could go. I know Terry and Roger are ready."

"As long as you clean 'em, Mr. Hughes. I'm not cleaning catfish."

The river was at its lowest in July and August, making it easy to seine for minnows. Lines were set above the drifts and baited. The men built a fire from driftwood.

"It's a fun thing. I really enjoy trotlining. I appreciate you fellows inviting me along. It makes me feel like I am a part of the community, and I haven't been here a month."

"You are a part of the community, Terry. A very important part, I might add. We think you are an excellent replacement for Reverend Crampton, and that takes some doing. The old gent has the respect of everyone in town. He is well known throughout Southern Oklahoma and North Texas. I guess he knows most all the preachers in that area, and they have called on him to conduct revivals in their churches. He's quite a guy."

"Yes, he is. He's sure been good to me since I've been here. I hope I can be half as good as he is."

"I have no doubt you will do fine. Everything we've heard has been good."

The conversation drifted from the school bond issue to the recent trial of Buster Phillips and the latest serial killing in Wichita Falls.

"Leroy and Howard took Buster to the state prison." Roy shook his head. "You'd think it was Howard that was going to the pen. Buster was his high school coach, and Howard thought Buster could do no wrong. I guess we really don't know what goes on in the mind of man."

Terry stared into space as if he was somewhere else. "No, I guess we really don't. Sometimes it just seems a man loses a grip on himself. Of course I never knew Buster Phillips, but I have seen this type of thing before. I know I almost lost my mind when I lost my wife. She was a beautiful person, Roy."

"I'm sure she was."

"I guess the only thing I have to be thankful for is that I know where she is. She was a staunch believer. I know that Almighty God is guarding over her now, and she will be there when I get there. It's between here and there that sometimes becomes a problem for me. But I shouldn't burden you with my problem."

"That's what friends are for, Terry. Come, it's time to run the lines."

It was a good evening for fishing. The catch matched the previous trip. Fish would be in the frying pan tomorrow.

Saturday morning when Riley arrived at the office Roger had swept the floors and was melting the lead.

"This is gonna be a lot easier when fall gets here."

"Yeah. It's even better in the winter. I guess you got your share of cleaning catfish last night."

"Oh yeah. Mom has invited Reverend Williams for dinner. Uncle Paul will also be there. It will be interesting to see how that goes."

"Well, I'm sure Paul will approve."

"I think so. Everybody I know likes the preacher."

"We have a couple small jobs for the job press. I'll take care of that, and you can set the governor's report and whatever else is on the copy hook. That ought to take up the rest of the morning. I guess you'll be in church in the morning."

Roger grinned. "I don't think Mom would let me miss if I wanted to."

Sunday morning's church service brought a surprise. Reverend Crampton was at the podium. Terry Williams was nowhere to be seen. John Crampton had a solemn look on his face."

"Reverend Williams is not with us this morning. He had to leave yesterday afternoon for Oklahoma City. His sister's father-in-law passed away, and he went to comfort the family and conduct the service."

After the service Riley caught up with Ruth Hayes as they were leaving the church.

"When did this happen, Ruth?"

"We had just finished dinner. I guess it was about four o'clock. Reverend Crampton knew Terry was at my house. He received the call from Terry's sister and called. Terry left immediately. Pretty sad."

"I guess Paul was impressed?"

Ruth smiled. "I see Roger has been keeping you abreast. Yes, Paul thinks he is a fine man. I guess I do, too."

"That's good. I think we all like him. Did he say when he is coming back?"

"No. I guess sometime this week."

It was not difficult to tell. Ruth had more than just a passing interest in Terry. Maybe, just maybe—in time.

# CHAPTER 22

When Riley returned to the office from his Monday visit at the "bench" and his advertisers, Joyce had some good news.

"The real estate office in Beaver Valley called, and they have sold the house in Madden Grove. That's been pressing on my mind, and I'm glad to see it sold. I didn't get quite what we were asking for, but it's not bad considering where it's at."

"Who is the world would want to move to Madden Grove?"

"It's an uncle of Katie's."

"Is he married?"

"I have no idea."

"If he's not, there could be a budding romance with Sybil directly across the street."

"Heaven forbid."

Roger was on his hands and knees picking up Linotype mats.

"Looks like you had an accident."

"I spilled the whole line. Second time I've done that this morning. I've spent more time on the floor than I have setting type."

"You are not the first one to do that and probably won't be the last. I guess I've done the same thing a hundred times. Has anybody heard from Terry?"

"He called Rev. Crampton last night and the reverend called Mom. He said the old gent had a heart attack while he was working in his garden. Apparently he died on the way to the hospital. He was seventy-four."

"I don't guess he said when he's coming back."

"Rev. Crampton didn't say."

"Another subject. We are going to have a large spread on the front page this week about the school bond election. I'll have it on the copy hook this afternoon. I guess I better take advantage of your typesetting since school starts next week. Looks like I am going to have to go back to work."

"I'll be here every afternoon to help and feed the press on Wednesday night's run."

"I don't see anything interesting coming down the pike this week. Seems something exciting seldom happens around here, and that's the way I like it. 'Mr. and Mrs. So and So went somewhere to see Somebody' is about it. I sometimes think we could take the personals and run them week after week and nobody would know the difference."

"I've noticed that. I guess that's what they want to hear."

Riley opened a can of cat food and filled Missy's bowl with milk. "Just like Missy here, everyone seems satisfied with the status quo. I can think of a lot worse things that can happen. Life in a small town has its advantages."

As Riley had predicted, it was another uneventful week. Thursday morning he made his usual trip to the post office with the weekly issue. Roy was sitting at the counter in Allen's Café when he arrived for coffee.

"Coffee for me, Mabel. What's up Roy? Don't tell me we have a big crime wave in the county, and I've missed it. I'd hate to be scooped by the *Beaver Valley Democrat.*"

"Not in the county Riley. I don't guess you've read the morning *Oklahoman.*"

"No I haven't. What are they predicting, another national championship for the University of Oklahoma?"

Roy frowned. "I wish that was all. Looks like the serial killer is on the loose again. Night before last they had a murder in Fort Worth and another in Oklahoma City last night. Apparently this guy is on the move."

"The police think it's the same guy?"

"From what the paper says, there are a lot of similarities. Alcohol was involved, and both of them were strangled with a rope."

"How many does that make?"

'Four in the Dallas area, two in Oklahoma City, one at Bowie and one in Wichita Falls."

"That's eight. Were any of the new victims sexually assaulted?"

"There were no indications that they had been; however, it won't be known for sure until they do an autopsy."

"I don't guess the FBI or the police are any closer to solving the last two than they are the first one?"

"You know they have to have some information. Obviously the modus operandi is the same in each case. Surely they were able to get some fingerprints, maybe there was some blood at some of the murders, or something. The guy is bound to have left something behind, some clue."

"You'd think so. Maybe he has, and the police aren't divulging what they have. If they publicize it, the killer may make some changes, not that you want another murder."

Roy pushed his cup forward as Mabel came with the refills. "I guess we're fortunate around here. When the big events in the county are a cakewalk, a rattlesnake hunt and a watermelon festival, I guess we pretty well have it made. A drunk now and then and sometimes a bad automobile accident, but the state troopers handle the accidents. I hope it stays that way."

"Let's hope so."

"Well, I gotta go down to Union Valley. Old man Pike's daughter has been trying for two days to call him and he doesn't answer the phone. She called the office in Beaver Valley, so I'll have to check it out. The old man is about half deaf, and unless he's sitting beside the phone, he isn't gonna hear it. This is the third time this year I've made a trip down there. The old codger needs to get a hearing aide."

Riley laughed. "Cheer up. You'll get old one of these days, and you probably won't hear any better than old Pike. I guess I better head back to the office and kill out this week's paper. This is the last full-time week for Roger until next summer, so I'll have to pick up the slack."

Rain in August in the Red River valley was not a common occurrence, but it did happen, and Thursday night was just such a time. Lightning and thunder accompanied by a torrential rain pelted the area well into the night.

"This ought to make the farmers happy, if it doesn't wash them away."

Joyce nodded. "At least we're not on the creek, like Madden Grove and Beaver Valley."

"If this keeps up, Red River will look like the Mississippi. I don't ever remember it raining this hard in the middle of August. I wonder if Terry made it home in this. I forgot to ask Roger. I would imagine Terry would have called Reverend Crampton or Ruth. Apparently he wasn't in town to conduct the Wednesday night prayer service, or Roger would have said something about it."

"I imagine he stayed a little longer than usual. That's pretty tough, and I imagine they are a close-knit family."

"Well, he'll probably be in tonight or tomorrow if he doesn't get flooded out along the way. If we can, I'd like to run over to Wichita Falls tomorrow. I noticed in one of the trade journals where one of the print shops has a font of 24-point mats for sale. That would give us another type size and style for the Linotype. They are about a fourth the cost of a new font, and we could use it. I don't have but two jobs for the job press, and I can handle that Saturday morning. Roger can man the shop while we're over there. We can take in a movie. What say you?"

"Sounds good. This rain reminds me of the time we met in Childress when a hard rain came."

"Yeah. I remember."

Riley placed his arm around Joyce. It would be a good night listening to the rain pelt against the window and for making love.

Saturday morning Riley stepped out of the shower. "Why don't we have breakfast at Allen's this morning? That way you won't have to cook."

"Golly, what's got into you? Your generosity overwhelms me."

A big grin crept across Riley's face. "Remember when you told me half of everything I have is yours?"

"So?"

"Then everything you have is half mine."

"What are you driving at?"

"Well if half of everything you have is mine, remember, you just sold your house in Madden Grove so I figure I can afford it this one time."

"You rascal." Joyce swatted him on the behind with a wet towel. "You don't pay me a salary for my hard work, and now you want half the money. Somehow I think I'm coming out on the short end of this deal."

"Yeah. But I love you. Riley pulled Joyce into his arms, still wet from the shower, and kissed her."

"I love you too, Riley, even if you are a bit soggy."

They both laughed and knew it would be a good marriage.

Allen's always served a good breakfast.

"I guess I better enjoy this. As tight as you are, I had almost forgot what the inside of a café looked like."

"Yeah, but you do such a good job, I almost hate to eat anywhere else but at your table."

"Baloney. And baloney is just what you might get for supper next week." Joyce drank from her coffee cup. "That is, if we have any baloney."

Mabel was taking it all in. She laughed. "If I didn't know better, I'd say someone was in deep trouble."

Riley winked. "She's a mean momma, but I love her anyway. I guess I better pay up, or I'll do well to get that baloney sandwich."

Beaver Valley was well named. The highway along Highway 70 on the south edge of town was all but under water as Beaver Creek was out of its banks.

"I guess we better come home across the Red River at Terral, or we may not make it back home. Another six inches, and the creek will be over the highway."

"I imagine it's just as bad in Madden Grove. The front yard will be knee deep."

Floods were a common occurrence along the Beaver but seldom in August. Most made their presence felt in the spring. A move was on to build a dam upstream, but it required congressional approval and federal funding, neither of which appeared forthcoming in the near future.

The usually placid Red River was bank to bank as Riley and Joyce crossed the bridge into Texas.

"I don't think we'll be trotlining in the river for a while. It's as high as I've seen it. It's a good thing there aren't any homes along the bank, or they'd be washed away."

Riley located the print shop in Wichita Falls. The Linotype mats were in fair shape and he would order a few replacements. Even so, it was a bargain and would be well worth the money.

"Now my dear, which movie would you like to see?"

"Peter O'Toole and Sophia Loren are starring in Man of La Mancha. That's about Don Quixote. I read the book. He's quite a character. I think I'd like to see that one."

"Then Man of La Mancha it will be. I might even fade for dinner after the movie."

A good movie and a good meal were like a short honeymoon. Wichita Falls sported several good Mexican cafés, and Riley selected a café on the second floor of a building overlooking a main thoroughfare.

Riley stared out the second story window as Joyce excused herself for the rest room. A familiar figure caught his eye crossing the street and opening a car door.

"It can't be him. It just can't. But it is."

Joyce returned from the restroom. "What's happened? You have the strangest look on your face. It's as though you're in another world."

"Maybe I am. You won't believe who I just saw getting into a car."

"Who?"

"None other than Farley Branson. He's supposed to be in South Texas working in a bank, and here he is in Wichita Falls. I don't believe it. Something tells me that Reverend Crampton knows more about this guy than he is telling. But why? Why the big secret?"

"Maybe you should ask him."

"Maybe I will."

# CHAPTER 23

"I thought you were going home through Terral instead of Beaver Valley. Remember the flood. We may not be able to get across the creek."

Riley turned the car around. "You're right. I guess I was preoccupied with Farley Branson. I just can't get over seeing him in Wichita Falls."

"Well, what if he isn't a banker in south Texas? Maybe he has his reasons."

"Yeah, but when he preached that Sunday, he wouldn't let me take his picture. It makes me think he's up to something."

"Like what?"

"I wish I knew. But I'm sure of this. Preacher Crampton knows more about him than he is letting on. He was talking with Rev. Crampton at the Watermelon Festival. It just doesn't add up. If he was a banker, he wouldn't be showing up in our town, at Terral, Duncan and now Wichita Falls."

"Whatever and whoever he is, I can't see that's so important. If Rev. Crampton knows him and he preached in the church, you'd think there is nothing wrong with him. Did Rev. Crampton tell you he was a banker?"

"No. It was Branson who said that."

"Are you going to talk to Rev. Crampton about this?"

"When and if the opportunity presents itself."

Riley was silent. Joyce moved to change the subject.

"Isn't the school bond election week after next?"

"A week from Tuesday."

"How do you think it will turn out?"

"I can't imagine the voters turning this one down. If they do, the state fire marshal will surely condemn the old building, and the school board will be struggling to find classrooms. I think the school board has presented a good case this time."

Riley sensed that Joyce had deliberately changed the subject. Maybe it was just the inquisitive instinct of a newspaperman, but he would not be satisfied until he knew more about Farley Branson. If Rev. Crampton knew Branson, he had to know he was not a banker in south Texas. But what was the connection between the good reverend and Branson?

Red River was running bank to bank when they crossed over the bridge at Terral.

"I'm sure Lake Texoma will catch a lot of water. I'll be glad when the river gets back to normal. I'd like to run trotlines again. We had pretty good luck the last two times. I'll be ready for a good catfish dinner by then."

"You catch 'em, and you're gonna be cleaning 'em. I'm not cleaning catfish or any other fish."

Riley grinned. "Yes ma'am. I'll drop you off at the house. I have a couple small jobs to do at the office, and I'll check with Roger and see if anything has come in."

Roger had completed pouring the lead pigs for the next edition and had swept and cleaned the shop. Riley thought the shop looked much better since Roger came to work—no paper was scattered around the floor and everything was in its proper place. His mother had taught him well.

"Anything new come in?"

"Yes. We got a half page ad in the mail from Wilson's Office Supply in Duncan. Other than that, nothing."

"Did Terry make it in?"

"Yes. He called Mom about the middle of the morning. He said he would be conducting the service tomorrow. Guess you'll be there?"

"Yeah. He does a good job, preaches a good sermon and he doesn't take all morning to do it."

"He's really a good preacher. I know Mom really thinks so."

"Maybe she likes him more than just his preaching."

"You may be right about that. He seems to feel the same about her. I know Mom seems a lot happier these days."

"That's good. People were not meant to live alone, Roger. I know it is a little early yet, but maybe things will work out for the two of them. Your mother is a nice looking lady, and Terry seems like a great guy. What does your uncle think?"

"I haven't heard him say but I can't imagine why he would object."

"And you?"

"If that's what Mom wants, well, I guess that's her decision."

"I guess it is."

"School starts Monday. We get out at three o'clock, so I'll be to work after that."

"Okay. After you sweep out, you should still have time for an hour or so on the Linotype. You are coming along quite well, and by this time next year you'll be as good as a seasoned pro."

Printing envelopes, letterheads, invoices, checks and other similar jobs were not Riley's favorite form of work, but they were necessary to augment the sometime slim earnings of a weekly newspaper. The old hand fed job press had seen better days, but it would have to do, at least for the time being. Business hardly justified investing in more modern equipment.

Riley knew that the declining population in rural America would have a detrimental effect on small towns and weekly newspapers. Perhaps in another generation or two weekly newspapers would be few and far between. He had often considered another profession but knew as long as his father was alive, it would be difficult to change. The old man simply believed things would always be as they were, but Riley could see the handwriting on the wall. Be that as it may, Riley finished the two small jobs, cleaned the press and fed Missy.

"Girl, behave yourself. Don't go tom-catting around, and I'll see you Monday."

Joyce was washing clothes.

"What's to eat?"

"Is that all you think about, something to eat?"

"A hard working man gets hungry."

"You had enough for lunch to feed a horse."

"That doesn't answer my question. What's to eat?"

"A baloney sandwich. That's what to eat."

"Here I thought I had married the best cook in the county outside my mother, and you offer up a baloney sandwich."

Joyce laughed. "I guess I fooled you, didn't I?"

Riley pulled Joyce into his arms and kissed her. "I love you, and you do make the best baloney sandwiches in the county."

"Thanks for the compliment. You smell like printer's ink."

"I wonder why that is." Riley grinned. "I guess I was born smelling like printer's ink. I'll hit the shower so I'll be ready for church in the morning. I wonder what Terry will preach on tomorrow. And I may get a chance to talk to John Crampton about Farley Branson. I just can't seem to get it off my mind."

Terry's Sunday sermon was family oriented. The recent experience in his own family brought home a need to show love on a daily basis for family members.

"You never know when tragedy will strike. My sister's father-in-law seemed to be in excellent health. One minute he was alive and active, and the next minute he was gone."

There was a long pause after that sentence, and Riley could almost sense he was thinking of his own personal loss. His pain might decrease over time, but Terry would never forget the loss of his wife.

After the sermon, Terry made his way to the exit as Sister Charlotte played "Amazing Grace" on an antique organ. Terry shook hands with the men and nodded at the ladies as they left the church.

"I thought you might get flooded out on your way home."

"No, Riley, it must have moved south. I noticed some of the creeks were running full, but the roads were clear."

"I don't see Rev. Crampton. He was here a minute ago."

"Terry smiled. "He isn't going to miss church on Sunday morning, but he left for home as soon as it was over. He and his wife are planning on spending a couple weeks in Colorado. I guess the old gent is entitled to a vacation. No telling how long it has been since he has had one."

"I'm sure that's right."

Farley Branson would just have to wait.

# CHAPTER 24

"Maybe this Branson guy is a bank examiner working for the federal government. Since he shows up in all these towns and claims to be the vice president of a bank, he may be using that to cover his real job."

"Ye gads, Riley. You're going to worry yourself into the grave trying to figure out something that probably doesn't amount to a hill of beans, and a small hill at that."

"Well, maybe so. But I'm gonna find out sooner or later."

Joyce shook her head. "The big bond election is coming up next week. Right now that's a lot more important than Farley Branson, whoever he is."

"You're right. I'm planning on devoting most of the front page to it. I plan on playing up the New London explosion back in the thirties. I just can't see anyone voting against it, though I know a few who will. I can't think of anything more important than the safety of the children in the community."

"That's for sure."

"I guess I'll make the rounds. I know we had a full paper last week, and this will be the last week before the bond issue, so we will have additional advertising. We'll have a full paper this week. I had hoped we would escape one week without an obituary, but such is not to be. I'll drop by Tom's and get the obit on Harrison Edwards. I hear he passed night before last at the rest home. Seems like that is the last stop for a lot of people."

"I'm sure it is. I guess we can be thankful there is such a place. At least they have someone to take care of them. It makes you wonder what we did before we had rest homes."

"I guess their families took care of them. It's just that some of these folks in the rest home don't have families. They have outlived them. Mr. Edwards must have been in his early nineties."

Tom was sitting behind his desk when Riley entered the funeral home.

"Looks like we lost another old timer now that Harrison is gone."

"You are one short, Riley. Maggie Smothers died early this morning."

"Golly, Tom. We're losing 'em faster than we're gaining. I think the last birth was two weeks ago. At this rate, the town in going to dry up."

"It's the same with all small towns. It seems most of the young folks are moving to the big cities to find work. There's not much to do around places like this, unless you farm, and even the farmers are fewer than they used to be. It's sad Riley, it really is."

"I've thought about just such as that here of late. Fewer people mean less business. I know a couple of the stores are barely hanging on, and I wouldn't be surprised to see them gone in a year or two. The newspaper isn't exactly a gold mine. I've considered doing something else, and if it wasn't for Dad I might well do it. He thinks things will always be the same. I could probably make more money working for a daily newspaper somewhere."

"I'm sure you could, but small towns do have certain advantages. We have very little crime, and if someone strays from the norm, everyone knows about it. I remember playing hooky and going fishing when I was in the ninth grade. My dad knew about it before I got home. I never made that mistake again."

Riley laughed. "Yeah. I guess Maurine is our biggest criminal, at least our most regular. When she gets too much to drink, she's a hell raiser. Roy says she's as tough as any man he's ever had to arrest, and he usually has to have some help."

"She's a real terror."

Riley grinned. "Wasn't she your girl friend in high school? I understand you proposed to her, but she turned you down."

"I ought to throw you out of here."

"Before you do, give me the obits and your ad supporting the school bond issue. This will be the last issue before the election."

"A few more cracks like that one, and they'll be reading your obit." Tom poked Riley in the ribs. "Go ahead and make up an ad for me on the school bond issue. Now get outta here before I give you more than a punch in the ribs."

The school bond issue was an easy sell for the second week. Merchants would be out front in their support. Even the rest home placed a large advertisement promoting the bond issue, and a number of private citizens followed suit. At the end of the day Riley was sure the issue would pass.

"It looks like we'll have to go to twelve pages. The only other times we've done that are the graduation and Christmas issues. I wish school started a week later than it did. Roger is just going to have to work later than usual if we hope to get the paper out on time."

Joyce nodded. "I'll have to work extra hard to gather the news. I know we've got the Ogden-Martin wedding, and with school starting that will provide a little more. I'll do a story on the new history teacher. Extra work for me, too. I guess you'll fatten my paycheck this week."

"You're the highest paid reporter on the *Weekly Standard* as it is. You've got an inside line to the publisher, and you also have the best office in the building."

"I've got the only office in the building, and I'm married to the publisher."

"What more could you ask?"

"Keep on, Mr. Hughes, and you'll be eating baloney sandwiches the rest of the week, that is, if you're lucky."

Riley grinned as he bent over the desk and kissed Joyce. "Whatever you fix, my dear, is what we'll have."

It was as Riley predicted, a hard week. Both he and Roger worked well into the night Monday, Tuesday and Wednesday, and it was a relief to put the paper in the mail Thursday morning.

"A few more weeks like this one, and I'll be an old man. I can't remember working so hard. I don't think I could have made it without Roger."

"Yes, he is a good worker. Now that we have the week behind us, why don't we invite Roy and Phyllis and Terry and Ruth over for dinner Saturday night?"

"You're not paying cupid are you?"

Joyce grinned. "How could you tell, Mr. Hughes?"

"Women's minds work in strange and unusual ways, and I suspect you are no different than the average female. What are you planning on feeding them, baloney sandwiches?"

"No. We won't have any baloney left by the time you've eaten it all. I had bar-b-que in mind. Your mom tells me you are pretty good on the grill."

"You feed me baloney, and now you want me to cook. Some program you've got."

"I'll have to fix the salad, tea and the rest of it. You are getting off easy."

"Paper plates?"

"Sure. That way you won't have to wash dishes."

"You drive a hard bargain, Mrs. Hughes. I'll call Roy and Terry. You can call Ruth. It's a good idea. At the rate they are going, we may have a wedding on our hands one of these days. Besides, Roy and I will make a fisherman out of Terry."

"The church has been fortunate to have Rev. Crampton all these years, and I'm thinking Terry is the ideal replacement. He might just want to make this his home."

"Particularly with Ruth around?"

"Now you're thinking ahead of the game. They seem to be a perfect match. I know the two of them have had some lonely times. Ruth has had to raise Roger by herself with a little help from her brother, and Terry lost his wife sometime back. It just seems a good match."

"You may be right. I have a couple small jobs to do Saturday morning, but I should be through before lunch. I'll clean up the old grill."

Roy never turned down a meal. "Phyllis and I will be there. Howard is coming down to make the rounds with me this afternoon. We've got to make a run down to Terral, but I should be through by five o'clock. We'll be there around six. Do I detect a little push for Terry and Ruth?"

"You are quite perceptive. I think when it comes to romance, women never miss a beat, and Joyce is no exception. See you around six."

At precisely six o'clock, Terry and Ruth arrived as the phone was ringing.

"It's for you, Riley. It's Roy."

It was a very short conversation.

"Roy said he would be about fifteen minutes late. Apparently something happened."

Riley and Terry sat on the patio as the two women were preparing the table. Riley turned the meat on the grill.

"Smells good. It's been a long time since I've had bar-b-que." Terry looked away from the grill as if his mind was somewhere else. "I used to bar-b-que quite a bit. I guess the last time was about a week before I lost my wife. It brings back some good memories."

"I'm sure it does."

"I don't guess you ever forget something like that, but I am doing a lot better with it now. Ruth has made quite a difference."

"She's a good person. She's had it pretty tough raising Roger by herself."

"He's a fine young man. She did well."

Roy and Phyllis arrived. Roy's arm was bandaged and he sported a small cut on his forehead.

"Ye gads, Roy. What happened to you?"

"Maurine."

"Maurine?"

Roy grimaced. "Yeah, Maurine."

"What's she done this time?"

"She was drunk and raising the roof at the bar. We had to haul her up to Beaver Valley to the jail. If Howard hadn't been with me, I don't think I could have made it by myself. Man, she is one tough female. I bet she could outfight most men. She has the foulest mouth of any person I know, men included."

"Maybe the judge will salt her away for a while."

"For public intoxication? Not hardly. She'll be out in a day or two. One of these days she is gonna have an accident and either kill someone or herself."

Terry shook his head. "That's sad. Has she always been like that?"

"Well," said Riley, "I went to school with her. She certainly wasn't the valedictorian, but then neither was I. I don't know what happened to her. It seems when she gets full of beer she gets mean, as Roy can testify."

"That I can, Mr. Hughes. I must say, she took it all out of me. I'm famished. I do guess you are planning on feeding us before I drop from starvation."

Riley laughed. "You're always hungry. It'll be ready in a few minutes."

The conversation turned to trotlining and the men planned another fishing trip to the river. Riley gathered the meat from the grill, and dinner was served.

It was a good evening for visiting. Joyce was indeed quite perceptive. When Terry and Ruth looked at each other their feelings were obvious. Love was beginning to blossom.

# CHAPTER 25

The big day finally arrived. The polls were open, and Riley and Joyce were among the first to cast their ballots in the school bond election.

"I know it will pass this time. It's just by how much. What is your prediction?"

"At least three to one in favor." Joyce thought it might go by an even larger margin. "Maybe four to one. I can't see how anyone could vote against this."

"There's Rev. Crampton standing over by the post office. Now is my chance."

"What chance?"

"To find out a little more about Farley Branson."

Joyce frowned. "For goodness sake. Go over there and ask him and set your mind at ease. Good grief."

Riley walked the short distance to the post office, and John Crampton was thumbing through his mail.

"Hey, Reverend, I thought you were in Colorado."

"I was, Riley. We decided to come back a day or two early so we could vote in the school bond election. What's new?"

"Well, for one thing, Joyce and I were in Wichita Falls a week or so ago and guess who we saw?"

"I have no idea."

"Farley Branson."

"So?"

"Well, Rev. Crampton, I've run into him here, at Terral, Duncan and now Wichita Falls. It's hard to believe he is a banker in south Texas when he shows up all these different places."

"A banker, eh? Is that was he told you?"

"Yes sir, and I find it hard to believe. How long have you known him?"

"Let me see now. Not for very long—only a day or so before he preached at the church."

Riley was puzzled. "Did he tell you he was a banker?"

John Crampton was ill at ease. "No Riley. He didn't tell me he was a banker. Why is that so important, one way or the other?"

"Well, Rev. Crampton, I don't know as it's important. It just seems to me a little hard to believe. He just doesn't seem to fit the mold. He seems more like a bank examiner than a banker."

"Maybe he has his reasons for telling you that."

"Maybe so, but I thought you might be able to shed a little light on the subject."

"Rest assured, Riley, that he is an honest man. As he mentioned in church, he is not a preacher by profession, but his father is. As to his being a banker, that's just something you will have to discuss with him."

John Crampton was becoming a little annoyed, and Riley detected it. Better to let the subject drop. Riley was more curious than before, but it was time to change the subject.

"What's your prediction on the school bond issue?"

"I think it will pass rather easily. The last time we had such an election the school board did not do a good job selling the bond issue. With the threat of closure of the old building by the state fire marshal and their campaigning, it should be an easy sell. And, by the way, the contribution made by the *Weekly Standard* didn't hurt either."

"We'll know by seven o'clock tonight. By the way, Ruth and Terry, along with Roy and Phyllis were over Saturday night for bar-b-que. I am beginning to think Terry and Ruth are getting serious."

"I have spoken to him on the matter. He is a lonely man, and I know Ruth is lonely, too. They seem to be compatible. Maybe things will work out for the two of them."

"I hope so. Enjoyed talking to you. I guess if I ever run into Farley Branson again, I'll just have to approach him directly."

John Crampton's face sported a wry grin. "That's what I would do, Riley. Whenever I wanted to know something, my dad always told me to go directly to the source."

Back at the office Joyce asked: "Well, did you find out about Farley Branson?"

Riley shook his head. "I know John Crampton knows what he does, but he wouldn't say. He told me if I wanted to know to ask Branson the next time I see him."

"That sounds logical to me."

"Well, life goes on. I'll have to make the rounds. We probably won't have a lot of news this week outside of the bond election. I suspect the advertising may also be a little short. I've been thinking, Joyce."

"About what?"

"Well, the *Weekly Standard* has been in the family for over forty years now. I don't know anything else but the newspaper. I can remember when we had more advertising than we do today. Molly's Dress Shop and Wimpy's Service Station are not the most profitable institutions around, and I wouldn't be surprised if they both folded within a year."

"What are you driving at, Riley?"

"Like I said, the paper has been in the family for a long time, and Dad thinks it will always be the same. With the decline of business in town, we may be hard pressed ourselves to make a go of it."

"What do you propose we do about it?"

"Both of us have newspaper experience. I am thinking we might make it better working for one of the large dailies. The paper still belongs to Dad, but he can't run it any more. I don't know how much longer we can make it, and I dread the time I have to face Dad and tell him it's time to sell. Sell, that is, if we can find a buyer."

"That's your decision. This has been your home all your life. You grew up here, know all the people, and that counts for a lot."

"Yes, I know. All my friends are here and you have some, too. I guess we can hang on until we have to make a move. I am not looking forward to it, but somehow I know it's coming."

Riley found Missy standing near her empty bowl.

"I guess that means you want something to eat?" Riley picked Missy up and, with a little petting, the purring started. "Let's see what we can do about that."

Riley opened a can of cat food and poured milk from the refrigerator. He sat at the Linotype and watched Missy eat, thinking how some animals had it made. They never had to worry about where the next meal was coming from; they just knew it would be there. He watched as Missy finished eating and began to rub against his leg. Riley picked the cat up, sat her in his lap and started the Linotype. His thoughts were of his conversation with Joyce concerning the newspaper. Uncertainty about the future was a cause for concern, and at some point in the future Riley knew he would have to make a decision.

There were only two polling places in the community, and it would not take long to count the ballots. Riley and Joyce remained in the office until the results were in.

"Looks like you hit it pretty close. Four to one in favor."

Joyce nodded. "I'm surprised it didn't pass at an even higher rate."

"There are always a few folks who would vote 'no' if it was free of any tax. It's just the nature of some."

"I wonder what's next."

"No telling. Not much happening in the old town. We could use a little excitement around here."

"Sometimes you get more than you bargained for—best not to ask."

# CHAPTER 26

The dog days of summer drifted into autumn. Fall, winter and early spring were usually pleasant in southern Oklahoma and north Texas. Leaves of the blackjack trees slowly began to turn a rusty color, and the mesquite trees would hold on beyond the first freeze. Mesquites were not native to the area but were transported many years past from Mexico. It was a constant battle by area farmers to rid their pastures of the pesky mesquite.

It was business as usual at the *Weekly Standard.* Fall advertising was less than Riley had hoped, and, had it not been for legal advertising and want ads, it would have been a bleak time. As Riley had predicted, Molly's Dress Shop was going out of business with a final sale. Molly was approaching her seventieth birthday and had run the business for thirty years, but with the decline in population and her advanced age, it was time to make a move.

"I almost hate to close up, Riley. I've been here now for just over thirty years, and it's been my life. I've met a lot of good people here, and it breaks my heart to close, but business is not what it once was, and I am not as young either."

"What are your plans Molly?"

"Since Fred died I have no one here. I have two daughters and a son. The daughter in Abilene, Texas has invited me down to stay with her. I think that's what I will do. It's a much bigger town with better medical facilities, and when you get my age that's a consideration."

"I understand, Molly, but I hate to see you go."

"And I hate to go Riley, but there comes a time." Molly smiled. "I will take the paper and keep up with the happenings around here."

As Riley walked back to the newspaper office he wondered what he would be doing when he reached seventy, that is, if he ever reached seventy. It once again brought to mind the gradual decline in both the business community and in population. He thought of three farm families who sold their property and moved to larger cities.

"You have a rather sad look on your face, Riley. What's the matter?"

Riley looked at Joyce and then out the front window as if he was somewhere else. "It's Molly Dunbar. She's closing the dress shop and moving to Abilene, Texas. It's more than losing a regular advertiser. It's like losing a part of your family. I've known Molly since I was in grade school. It's sad. It really is."

"Is she selling the store, or just closing it?"

"She said she is having a sale to try to sell most of her stock. She said Martin's Dry Goods at Beaver Valley would buy the rest. At least I guess you can find some bargains."

"Women always welcome bargains, but I would rather it be some other way."

Riley retired to the back office and flipped the switch on the Linotype. It was Missy's signal for petting.

"Is Riley in?"

"Yes. He's in the back office, Roy."

"What's up, Roy?"

"I thought you would like to know. They've had another murder in the Dallas area. She was strangled with a rope, but the police seem to have some question as to whether or not it is the work of the serial killer. They didn't give a lot of details. Apparently whoever did it has been following the serial killer's modus operandi and is trying to lay the blame at his feet."

"What's so different?"

"For one thing, there was no handwritten note."

"I didn't know there were handwritten notes left in the other murders."

"Neither did I, until today. I don't know why they would withhold that type of information. That is a good clue if they can ever find a match. It may be they have a suspect. The report we got is that several people have been questioned but nothing beyond that.

"Oh, yeah. The police did solve the murder in Fort Worth. The guy killed his wife. Apparently she had been seeing another man, and he caught up with her. She had been to a local bar, and he waited outside. When she came out, he strangled her. That would account for the alcohol. The autopsy was like the rest, no sexual assault. One of the neighbors said there had been a lot of strife between the two."

"I don't guess the police are any closer to catching the serial killer than they were two months ago. It makes you wonder when he will strike again. You've got to wonder what motivates that guy. He must have a vendetta of some kind. Maybe he's just plain psycho."

"Who knows? I know he's got the entire area from Oklahoma City to Dallas wondering where and when he will strike next. It's not a good feeling."

"No, it's not."

"AA has asked the paper in Beaver Valley and over at Ringling to print something on it and wants you to do the same. I doubt anything like that will ever happen in a community as small as ours, but you never know. Stranger things have happened."

"We'll be glad to do it. Let me know if AA needs anything else down here. I guess you heard. Molly is closing her dress shop after thirty years."

"No, I hadn't heard."

"That will be another empty building on Washington Street. Maybe someone will put something in there. It's a pretty nice building."

"Let's hope so. Have you heard from Terry or Ruth lately?"

"I see them in church every Sunday. Roger keeps me posted. I wouldn't be surprised if he doesn't pop the question one of these days."

Roy laughed. "I guess Joyce is putting more wood on the fire every chance she gets."

"Typical female. You know it."

"Well, I've got to go down to old man Pike's house again. His daughter has been trying to call him for three days now, and he doesn't answer. The telephone company is either going to have to put a siren on his phone, or he is going to have to get a hearing aid, and a loud one at that. He's as hard headed as he is deaf."

Riley laughed. "Things are pretty slow around here. Time to give some thought to another fishing trip."

"I'm ready. I know Terry is, too. I think that guy can eat his weight in catfish."

"Next time I see him, I'll tell him you said that."

It was an uneventful week. Riley took the paper to the post office on Thursday.

"I'm rum-dumb. Let's go to Beaver Valley and see if Ben still has a good chicken fried steak. I don't know what's showing at the Empress, but we might take that in if it's worth seeing."

"Sounds good to me. I'm going to Molly's to see what she has on sale. I need a new dress or two and a pair of shoes. Some of my clothes are threadbare, and if I don't get some new shoes, I'll have to go barefoot. You wouldn't want people to think you were so tight you wouldn't fade for a new dress or two now and then would you?"

"I guess that means you want the checkbook."

"You are becoming more and more perceptive, Mr. Hughes."

"Women. If you get many more clothes, I'll have to hang mine on the back porch, that is, what few I have."

Joyce held out her hand as Riley reached for the checkbook. Handing her the checkbook, he laughed. "Now get outta here before I change my mind."

"Remember the baloney sandwiches."

"Yes, ma'am."

Riley watched as Joyce stepped out the door on her way to Molly's.

"Women. I don't guess I will ever understand them and clothes. I could wear denim trousers, a shirt and the same shoes every day. Seems like I have heard Dad say the same thing a hundred times."

As slow as business was, Riley sat back in his chair and was soon asleep. He woke to the opening of the front door.

"Wake up lazy bones. You won't be able to sleep tonight if you sleep all afternoon. Look at the dresses I bought. What do you think?"

Riley wouldn't know a good dress from a bad dress, but he knew better than to do anything but compliment Joyce on her selection. "They're really nice. I particularly like the blue one. Were there a lot of women in Molly's checking out the bargains?"

"No, not really. Ruth was there. Golly, she is as happy as I have seen her. She reminds me of a high school girl readying for her first date. It's pretty obvious that she really likes Terry. Maybe love is a better word. If he feels the same way, matrimony may be just around the corner."

"I've been thinking the same thing. Let's call it a day. There is nothing happening around here that Roger can't handle. I'm not even sure I have any work for Saturday. I guess Roger can set some extra type. We may have to have it to fill up the paper as short as we are on advertising."

It was as Riley thought it would be, a slow Saturday morning. Roger poured the lead pigs and spent the rest of the morning setting type.

After feeding Missy, Riley told Roger to lock up and left for the house. He would cut the grass, hopefully for the last time until spring, take a shower and take Joyce to Beaver Valley for Ben's chicken fried steak.

The movie was a re-run they had seen before. "I've got a good western to read, so that'll take up the evening for me."

"I think I'll run up to Madden Grove and visit with Katie. It's been a while since I've seen her, and she can fill me in on what's going on. Maybe I might even get a little news, sure enough if I run into Sister Lang."

Riley sat back in his easy chair, completely absorbed in a western. It was as though he was actually there, working on a ranch in New Mexico in the 1870s. When Joyce arrived home he had just finished the novel. It was bedtime, and Riley lay in bed thinking how life must have been before the conveniences of his time. No automobiles, no radio, no telephones, just a simple way of life. He would carry the novel into his dreams.

He awoke with Joyce shaking his arm.

"Get up Riley. It's Roy. He's on the phone."

"For gosh sakes. What time is it?"

"It's one o'clock in the morning. Wake up."

Riley stumbled into the kitchen, still half asleep. It suddenly dawned on him that Roy would not be calling at one o'clock in the morning if it was not important.

"Hello. What's happened, Roy?"

"You better get dressed and get to the hospital."

Riley was now wide-awake. "What's the problem?"

"It's Terry. He's called for you two or three times. You need to get up here in a hurry."

"Is he hurt?"

"Just come on. I'll tell you when you get here."

Joyce was standing in the doorway. "What's happened?"

"I don't know. Roy said to come to the hospital. It's Terry. He didn't say what happened, but I needed to get there in a hurry. I'll either call you from the hospital or tell you when I get back."

Riley donned his clothes and hurried to the car. A thousand questioned ran through his mind. What happened to Terry?

# CHAPTER 27

Riley drove the ten-mile trip to the county hospital along a rain soaked highway. He couldn't imagine what had happened to Terry. Had he been in a serious auto accident? That was the only thing he could think of, and he wondered if Terry was seriously hurt. He arrived at the hospital and Roy was in the lobby waiting for him.

"What happened, Roy?"

"You're not going to believe this. He's been stabbed and is in critical condition."

"Stabbed? For God's sake, who would want to stab Terry Williams? The man never did anything to hurt anyone."

"Maurine."

"Maurine? Why in the world would she stab Terry?"

"I'm not for sure. All the information I have is what she told me. I was about to check in for the night when AA called. He said he had received a call from Maurine and that she was about half drunk, as usual. She said she had just stabbed a man with some scissors when he tried to strangle her. He told me to go to her place and check it out.

"When I got there she was standing in her doorway. I asked her what had happened. She told me some guy had followed her home when she left the bar, and when she got out of the car he told her that she had killed his wife."

"Killed his wife?"

"That's what she said."

"Why would he say that?"

"I have no idea. She said he came at her with a rope in his hand and tried to strangle her. She had a pair of scissors in her hand, and she stabbed him. She said she ran in the house and called the office. AA was working late and answered the phone. He told me to check it out. He didn't seem too concerned at the time. Maurine has pulled some pretty wild stuff and he thought she was just on one of her drunks."

"Where is Maurine now?"

"I took her to the office in Beaver Valley. AA is questioning her. He told me to stand by here at the hospital. Maurine had blood on her clothes when I took her in."

"How did Terry get to the hospital?"

"I guess he drove himself."

"Have you talked to him?"

"Only for a minute. They ran me out of the room. Apparently the scissors must have pierced a vital organ. It doesn't look good, Riley."

"I wonder why he called for me?"

"He called for you, me and John Crampton. I guess we are the best friends he has. I didn't call Rev. Crampton. He's not as young as he once was, and I'm afraid he might have a heart attack if I called him this time of night. He'll find out soon enough. Obviously, Terry won't be there for services later this morning. I guess someone will have to tell Rev. Crampton later in the morning."

"What do you think Roy? Do you think Maurine is telling the truth?"

"Well, it certainly looks like it. Even she doesn't go around stabbing people."

"And she said Terry told her that she killed his wife?"

"That's what she said."

"Maurine doesn't even know his wife."

"I know that. I've been thinking Riley about this. It sure bears a lot of similarities to the serial killings. You don't suppose…?"

"Terry? How could it be him? He is as gentle a soul as there is."

"You are right about that. Even so, we'll have to check it out. AA has called the night number of the FBI in Dallas. I'm sure they will send someone up here to check it out. They should have some fingerprints or something from some of the other murders. They can get Terry's prints and that will probably clear him. At least I hope so. Remember, they have some handwriting samples, and it will be easy to get some of those from Terry's office."

"And Maurine said that he came toward her with a rope in his hand and told her that she killed his wife?"

"Yeah. She said he said it over and over, four or five times."

"Terry told me his wife died in an auto accident."

"You know Maurine had nothing to do with it."

Rita Martin entered the lobby from a side door. "Riley, he insists on seeing you. It doesn't look good. He has lost a lot of blood. You can only stay for a minute."

Rita led Riley to the emergency room. Terry was lying on a blood-soaked bed. His eyes were glazed and he held out his hand as Riley walked to the bed.

Terry Williams was delirious. "I had to do it, Riley," he whispered. "She won't kill again. She killed my wife. But she won't kill again." Terry kept saying it over and over. "She killed my wife. She killed my wife. Don't you see? She killed my wife."

"When did she kill your wife Terry?"

Terry was searching for an answer. "I don't know. Maybe it was yesterday."

"How, Terry, how?"

Tears were streaming down his cheeks. "In the parking lot. In the parking lot. She was drunk, and she ran over my wife in the parking lot."

Terry's voice was getting weaker and weaker. Rita was standing at the door.

"You better come out Riley. The doctor has just entered the hospital, and he'll be here in a minute."

Riley eased out the door, thinking it was sad that the county was so small and had so few doctors that they were on call instead of at the hospital to deal with such emergencies.

"We just as well have a cup of coffee and wait." Roy poured two cups from the coffee urn in the lobby. "What did he have to say?"

"He kept saying she killed his wife. I asked him how. He said Maurine ran over her in the parking lot."

"We don't even have a parking lot, except at the school, and his wife has been dead for quite some time. I'll tell you what I think, Riley. I think whoever ran over his wife was a drunk female, and when he sees one, he thinks she is the one. Why else would he pick Maurine out? "

"That's a possibility. It won't be hard to find out for sure how his wife died. That is strange. I feel sorry for the guy. Whenever he sees a drunk female in a car I guess he loses it altogether."

"We may be jumping to conclusions."

Riley stared into his coffee cup. "Hard to believe, hard to believe. What is AA going to do with Maurine?"

"Not much he can do. I imagine she's as sober as the judge is right now. I called the office while you were in with Terry. AA said she was sober, and it was the first time he had ever seen her cry. Apparently she is pretty well tore up over it. He said he would take a statement from her, and when he got through I could take her home. She's not going anywhere. There is no need to hold her."

"This is really going to be hard for Ruth."

"Yeah. It sure is. I'd hate to be the one to have to tell her."

"I guess that job will go to John Crampton. I imagine he's done it a hundred times before, maybe not under these circumstances."

"Preachers get a lot of flack from people, mostly unjustified. Whatever, I sure wouldn't want to be in John Crampton's shoes. This is going to be extra tough."

"What time is it?"

"Two-thirty."

A nurse came from a back room. "You're wanted on the phone, Roy."

Roy disappeared behind the lobby door. Riley poured another cup of coffee and walked to the window facing the street below. He lifted the cup to his lips, wishing this was not really happening. How could Terry Williams do such a thing? And what if it turned out that he was responsible for all the other murders? He began to think back. Terry was in Oklahoma City for his sister's father-in-law's funeral when the last murder took place. The murder in Fort

Worth the day before had been solved by the Fort Worth police. Even so, that could just be a coincidence.

Roy entered the lobby. "That was AA. He took a statement from Maurine and told me to come to the office and pick her up and take her home. He said he was going home and would be at the hospital at eight in the morning. That's when the special agent from the Dallas FBI office is due in. He did say they had some latent fingerprints from some of the past murders, and he would bring them and make a comparison."

"I'll stay here until daylight in case something happens. Then I guess it's my job to tell John Crampton. I'll do that, stop by the house, and then I'll be back up here by the time AA and the FBI agent gets here. Are you coming back up?"

"Not tonight. I think I'll try to get some sleep. I'll be back early in the morning. I don't know what AA will want me to do, but right now I'm dead on my feet. It was a long day even before all this happened. I'll see you later in the morning."

Riley sat on a couch in the lobby and was soon asleep. He was awake at six when a nurse was rattling the coffeepot. Rita was standing at the front desk talking to the receptionist.

"How is Terry? Is there anything new?"

"No. He's still hanging on, but that's about it. He falls in and out of consciousness. I'm afraid the doctor doesn't give him much chance."

Riley still couldn't believe Terry Williams tried to strangle Maurine. Yet he knew it was so. The more he thought about it, the more convincing was the evidence against Terry Williams. He was in the Dallas and Fort Worth area where he had a small church in a nearby town. He could well have been in Oklahoma City visiting his sister during the first murder in that city. He could easily have been going through Bowie when that homicide occurred. That left only the one in Wichita Falls and it was just a short journey there. It didn't look good.

He drove to John Crampton's home and rang the doorbell. John Crampton was an early riser and had just finished breakfast.

"Goodness, Riley. You are up mighty early this morning. To what do I owe the pleasure of this visit?"

"I wish it was pleasure, Rev. Crampton. I'm afraid I'm the bearer of some very bad news."

"How's that, Riley?"

"Terry Williams is in the county hospital and it doesn't look like he is going to make it."

"What happened?"

"According to the information I got from Roy, he followed Maurine home from the bar last night and tried to strangle her. She stabbed him with a pair of scissors. I talked to him at the hospital for just a moment. He kept saying Maurine killed his wife, over and over. Maurine doesn't even know his wife."

"I'll tell my wife and go to the hospital."

"I was wondering, Rev. Crampton. Ruth doesn't know anything about this. It might be better if you told her. I hate to ask you to do that, but I'm not sure I can do it."

"I understand, Riley. I've done this type of thing many times before. It's not pleasant, certainly, but it goes with the territory. I'll stay with her as long as she needs me, and then I'll come to the hospital."

"Thanks. I'm going home to tell Joyce, and then I'll go back to the hospital."

Joyce was in her robe, sitting at the kitchen table when Riley arrived.

"I hardly slept a wink last night. What happened? How is Terry? Did he have an accident?"

"I'm afraid I have some bad news Joyce. Terry's in bad shape." Riley told of the events of the past night. "I'm afraid there is more to it than that."

"What do you mean?"

"You remember when Terry was in Oklahoma City, and the female was strangled under similar circumstances as the previous murders in the Dallas area?"

"Yes."

"It seems he could be in all those places where the murders occurred. And the victims are all females who had been drinking. He told me a drunk female ran over his wife in a parking lot. He told me he had to strangle Maurine so she would not kill again. He kept telling me over and over that she had killed his wife. I think he just lost control of himself when he saw a drunk female in a car and imagined that she had run over his wife."

"Does Ruth know about this?"

"No. Not yet. I stopped by John Crampton's on the way home and told him. He said he would take care of it. He said he would come to the hospital later. I guess his wife will have to meet with the congregation later this morning. It is really going to be a blow to them."

"I can imagine."

"I need to clean up and go back to the hospital. Terry was still hanging on when I left. I need something to eat."

"I'll fix breakfast while you clean up."

# CHAPTER 28

Riley sat at the table sipping coffee. "I can't believe it. It's just seems impossible, and yet everything in each of the murders points at Terry. It certainly is not for me to pass judgment, and I am hoping something will disprove what I am thinking. Maybe when the FBI agent gets here and takes his prints they won't match. He will probably also bring the handwritten notes left in the victim's cars. They can get samples from the church's office. I don't know anything about handwritten comparisons, but I understand they are about as positive an identification as fingerprints."

Joyce poured a second cup of coffee. "I guess we'll know something later in the day."

"Maybe so. Right now I'm worried about Terry. He was in terrible shape. He could barely speak when I was with him. Rita said he keeps falling in and out of consciousness and, according to her, the doctor didn't seem to give him much of a chance."

"That's awful. This is going to be a terrible blow for Ruth, even if he survives."

"Yes, I know. Rev. Crampton is with her now."

Riley finished his breakfast and took the last sip of coffee. "I guess I'll go back to the hospital. I know AA will be there, along with the FBI agent, when he gets here. I don't know what I'll be able to find out, but I'll let you know as soon as I can."

"Do you think I should call Ruth?"

"No. Let John Crampton stay with her for the time being. Maybe later. We'll just have to see what happens."

Riley checked his watch. It was eight-fifteen. The FBI agent was to be at the hospital by eight o'clock. He and AA should be there.

Riley backed the car out of the driveway. "What a mess!" he thought. "First it was Buster Phillips, and now this. If it turns out to be Terry, we'll have reporters from everywhere." He thought of a recent conversation with Roy. "Nothing much ever happens around here, and that's the way we like it."

When Riley arrived at the hospital, Roy was in the lobby.

"How's Terry?"

"Terry died an hour ago."

"Oh, my gosh. That's awful."

"Yes it is. The doctor did everything he could, but Terry had lost too much blood, and the wound was too severe."

"I'm still having a hard time believing Terry could strangle any one. It's just not like him to do something like that."

"I know Riley. I guess when he saw Maurine driving drunk, it just brought back memories of his wife and how she died, and he just snapped. I know, and you know that under normal circumstances there is no way he could do a thing like that."

"Did the FBI agent arrive?"

"Yes. He's back there now with AA. He's going to take Terry's prints."

"Did he bring the handwriting samples?"

"He didn't say."

"They may not have a handwriting expert in Dallas. They may have to send them to Washington."

"I'll call Joyce and tell her. She can contact Rev. Crampton and advise him. I imagine he is still with Ruth. Man! This is going to be a blow to her."

"You've got that right."

Riley went to the phone and called Joyce. "Terry passed away about an hour ago. You need to call John Crampton and advise him. The FBI agent is taking his fingerprints now. I don't know what will happen to Terry. I imagine Tom Smart will pick him up and call his sister in Oklahoma City."

There was a pause on the line. "No, I'll wait until the FBI agent and AA come out and talk to them. After that I'll come home."

Riley turned to Roy. "How long has AA and the FBI agent been back there?"

"About fifteen minutes. They ought to be coming out soon."

Roy poured two cups of coffee from the pot in the lobby. "We might as well have a cup of coffee while we wait."

"What are you going to do?"

"Not much I can do. I'll wait and see what AA wants me to do. I imagine I'll go into the office with him and see what I can find out about the fingerprints. I'll call you at the house when I find out anything."

AA appeared from behind the door leading into the back part of the hospital followed by the FBI agent, none other than Farley Branson.

"I knew it! I knew you were not a banker! But an FBI agent . . . ?"

"Yes Mr. Editor, I'm with the FBI office in Dallas. When you asked me what I did the first time we met, I was taken somewhat aback. Actually, my brother is a banker is south Texas."

"But why the big secret?"

"When you are working undercover, you are doing just that, and FBI agents do not want their pictures in the paper. I was assigned to this case by the senior agent."

"But what's the connection with Rev. Crampton?"

"He is well known throughout north Texas and southern Oklahoma. There were some indications from the notes left with the victims, plus a couple small Bibles in two of the cases, and we felt someone in religious circles might somehow be connected. We are still not sure, but when I make a fingerprint comparison we will know one way or the other if this Terry Williams had anything to do with it."

"But Rev. Crampton…?"

"Law enforcement seldom gets much done without help, and he agreed to keep my secret and keep his eyes and ears open. If this Terry is the one, I guess we all missed it."

"What do you think?"

"I won't know until we check the fingerprints. I'll have to send the handwriting samples to Washington. We don't have an expert in that area in Dallas. We're going to the sheriff's office now and I'll make a comparison."

Riley watched as Branson and AA left for the sheriff's office. He turned to Roy. "I knew it. I just knew he wasn't a banker, but I wouldn't have pegged him as a FBI agent. Even so, I can't see why the big secret."

"Sometimes you can learn a lot just by listening, particularly if someone doesn't know who you are."

"I'll go home. I guess everybody is gathering at the church now. I'm sure they will find this as hard to believe as we do. Gosh Roy, we went fishing with him, visited with him, and you would never in your wildest dreams believe he would commit murder. He seemed like as nice a person as you would ever want to meet."

"I guess he was, Riley. I know there is little room for forgiveness if he actually is the one, and I rather think he is. I guess the loss of his wife was more than he could bear, and a drunken woman in a car was the catalyst that set him off. I'll be down at the sheriff's office, and I'll let you know about the comparison."

Tears were streaming down Riley's cheeks as he drove toward home. Terry had made many friends in the community in the short time he had lived there. From all outward appearances, it seemed as though he was recovering somewhat over the loss of his wife, and with the love of Ruth, his life was looking much brighter.

Joyce was sitting at the kitchen table when Riley arrived.

"What's happened? What did you find out about the other murders?"

"Nothing yet. Roy said he would call. I did find out who Farley Branson was. He is an FBI agent out of the Dallas office. He took Terry's fingerprints and is at the sheriff's office making comparisons with the latent prints they found at the scene of the murders. Did you tell John Crampton?"

"Yes. He called his wife and had her come stay with Ruth. She is really upset. Rev. Crampton is at the church meeting with the congregation. He said his wife will stay with Ruth until her brother and his wife get there."

"I guess there is nothing to do but sit and wait for Roy's call. He said he would let me know as soon as he found out. Golly Joyce, this is the worst thing that has ever happened in this town.

Even if the prints don't match, we've lost a friend. And, in spite of the way she is, I imagine this is pretty tough on Maurine. You certainly can't hold her responsible if she was being attacked."

"I know this is a terrible ordeal for Ruth, but I'm sure Roger is taking it pretty hard. I know he was fond of Terry, but seeing his mother suffer is even worse."

It was the middle of the afternoon when Roy called.

"Bad news, Riley. Branson had three sets of fingerprints taken from three of the murders. Two of them matched. I guess that pretty well says it."

"Somehow I knew that was the way it was going to be."

"Branson said he would stop by Rev. Crampton's house on the way back to Dallas and see if he could get some handwriting samples out of the church office. Have you talked to Ruth?"

"No. Mrs. Crampton is with her. I understand Ruth's brother and his wife were on the way over."

"The news is already out—not about the other murders, but about Terry. I guess AA will have an office full of reporters tomorrow, especially when the word gets out that Terry has been identified as the serial killer."

"We have had our share of bad news this year, first Coach Phillips at Beaver Valley and now Terry. I wish I were doing something else, Roy. This has to be our lead story in next week's paper. I know everyone will have already read about it in the big dailies. Nonetheless, we'll have to cover it."

"If anything else develops, I'll be in touch."

"Thanks, Roy."

It would be a long week. Riley knew he would spend most of his time relating what information he had when he began his rounds Monday morning, starting with the bench.

"I almost hate to start the week."

Joyce agreed. "I imagine while you are uptown the phone will be ringing off the hook."

"Yes, and since we're the local newspaper I imagine we'll get a lot of traffic from the national news media, that is what the sheriff's office doesn't get."

Riley tossed and turned in bed. It would be a long, hard day. And it was as he suspected. Monday morning he was besieged by questions from the old timers at the bench. It didn't get much better when he made his morning rounds to his advertisers.

When Riley returned to the office, Joyce motioned to the back office. Roger was sitting at the Linotype holding Missy and staring at the machine. There were tears in his eyes.

"I didn't feel like going to school today. I just didn't. Mother cried yesterday and last night. I've thought about Rev. Williams all night. Why did he do it, Riley? He could have killed my mother."

"No Roger. Your mother was perfectly safe. It is not for me to say, and I am certainly no psychologist, but I'm sure Terry would never harm your mother. He was very fond of her."

"But why did he murder all those women?"

"I can't say for sure, but sometimes things happen that sets a man off. He wasn't the Terry Williams we knew when he committed those murders and tried to kill Maurine. He loved his wife as he loved your mother, and when he saw something that reminded him of how his wife died, he became an entirely different person."

"My mother is hurt. I don't know if she will ever get over this."

Riley placed his hand on Roger's shoulder. "No one in this community will ever forget what happened, Roger. I don't guess any of us understand totally why he did what he did, but it's done and there is nothing we can do to change it."

Tears were in his eyes as he looked up at Riley. "Yes, maybe in time."